CAN THE COXEMAN OVERCOME A TINY SILVER PILL?

Rod Damon finds the toughest opponent of his career in a harmless-looking pill—a pill with the power to turn men into sex machines, and women into love-hungry fiends!

The pill's effects are unbelievable. Every man immediately becomes an insatiable stud. His sexual powers know no limits. And the women just take it lying down!

But there is such a thing as too much of a good thing, and Rod must find the creator of the pill and destroy the formula—before the sexual balance of our whole civilization is screwed up!

T0352149

COXEMAN #17

THE BIG BROAD JUMP

AN ADULT NOVEL BY BY TROY CONWAY

POPULAR LIBRARY

Copyright © 1969 by Coronet Communication, Inc.

Popular Library
Hachette Book Group USA
237 Park Avenue
New York, NY 10017

Popular Library is an imprint of Grand Central Publishing. The Popular Library name and logo is a trademark of Hachette Book Group USA, Inc. The Coxeman name and logo is a trademark of Hachette Book Group USA, Inc.

Visit our Web site at www.HachetteBookGroupUSA.com

First Paperback Printing: December, 1969

Printed in the United States of America

Conway, Troy
Big Broad Jump, The / Troy Conway
(Coxeman, #17)

ISBN 0-446-54326-8 / 978-0-446-54326-2

CHAPTER ONE

"Mmmmmm . . . ."
  "Umph . . . ahhhhhh . . . ."
  "Oh! Oh! . . . . . ."   -
  "Ahhhhhhhhhhhhhh . . . ."
  "Ooooooooooooooooh . . . . ."

Mingled with all these usual sounds of sexual gratification were an assortment of grunts, groans and sighs. It was useless to try to decide whether the two women were enjoying themselves more than the two men. Or vice versa. Either way, all the graph charts on the small aluminum table in the Study Room were jitterbugging like mad. I hadn't seen the wired pens dance like that in days.

The Masters-Johnson technique of studied sexual response between the male and female of the human species has its champions. I, Rod Damon, am certainly one of them. I have always been interested, if that is the word, as to what exactly happens when Madame and Monsieur get together between the sheets, or above them. You might say it is my *raison d'etre,* what makes me tick, what runs my motor, and what makes me sing *Hallelujah!* I am a man first and a scientist secondly. Happily I have been able to coordinate both achievements, to the delight of my own existence and the enrichening of mankind's knowledge as regards Sex. And you don't have to be French to understand the thesis of Rod Damon. You have only to be a human being.

Like Suzanne and Annette and their two steaming, panting, piledriving paramours on the big wide table-bed in the heart of the room.

They didn't pay any attention to me at all. As they should not, of course. The subject was Research. I had wired their ankles and their hips with the sets of electrodes and circuit relays so that the graphs and charts before me could record their sexy efforts. Naturally, they were enjoying themselves. That was the whole idea or the project would be a frost. I am a scientist, as I said, not a *voyeur*. But just as Dr. Masters and Dr. Johnson found out, the viewing of males and females enjoying the world's greatest indoor (and outdoor) sport, does take its toll. The blood pressure count is all-important. It varies so much.

The Study Room was air-conditioned, uncluttered and subtly lit to induce relaxation and libertinism (my idea), and the two couples wildly copulating before my eyes had gone to town.

The pen tips were drawing racing, jagged lines on the charts; my own hands were racing to keep track of the progressive dips and rises on the graphs; and I was beginning to firm up myself in the old, familiar way. I cannot help it. I have priapism, and ever since I astounded the world of men and knowledge with my startling papers and books and experiments in Sexual Research, and founded L.S.D., The League of Sexual Dynamics, I have been a marked man. My capacity for love and lovemaking is ten times that of the average male, and since I am six feet two, well-conditioned and mentally solvent, I've been riding the gravy train ever since. The university which I made world-famous with my work honors me with a laboratory, a bachelor apartment and all the time and willing coeds I can desire. I desire a lot of them, but lately I had been spending a great deal of time in Theory, I must admit. Now I felt the old sensual yearnings of Practice assert themselves.

It was either Suzanne's fault or Annette's. It was hard to tell them apart in the writhing pile on the bed-table. One of them had the sauciest, most dimpled *derrière* in the universe, and she was using it like a weapon on the man beneath her. The couples had gone from formal fornication to Free-Style, and one of the worthies on the table (I never look at men) was being battered into submission. I wasn't surprised. It has been my experience that the average woman, given the time and the inclination, will outlast the average man. It is estimated that females average some fourteen orgasms, albeit minor, to the two or three savage blasts that males unload during a session. It's all quite simple, really. Women have the itch, men have to scratch it. Scratching does take more

6

physical effort. Or rather, the key has to move; the key-hole merely *is*. You see what I mean?

Anyway—the Masters-Johnson technique had been a roaring success. I'd had time to study one hundred couples in action. The university has classrooms busting and bursting with sexually starved students. Also, to study under the Great Damon is a stunning stimuli to Education in General. At the university, a student majored in Sex. There were the usual lot that wanted to be doctors, lawyers, engineers and journalists, but by and large my university turns out the Sexually Free and Uncomplicated graduate. And any one of them would have laughed right in the face of Mrs. Robinson. She couldn't have taught them anything like she taught Dustin Hoffman. The idea!

I wiped my hands on my white smock coat and put my pen down and turned off the switch on the graphs and charts and electrical outlets. The two couples did not cease in their efforts. Indeed, they were now skin-deep in the *ploy* I had suggested before they had taken their positions. The circular, clock-like revolvement around the center of things. The men seemed to find this hard to do but the twin females were having no trouble whatsoever. I call this the *Beat The Clock* method.

One of the partners lies still and supine beneath; the partner above (male or female) then merely lies on the love object and rotates, clockwise or counterclockwise in a complete circle. It is three hundred and sixty degrees of sheer delight, given the proper partners. Suzanne and Annette were now doing this with high glee. Their tanned, lithe bodies were finely dewed with animal perspiration. Their melon breasts and bell-shaped hips were gyrating wonderfully. But beneath them, the men had obviously reached their limit. I couldn't blame them, exactly. They had done pretty well for themselves. A glance at the watch on the desk showed me they had serviced Suzanne and Annette for nearly forty-five minutes. Not bad. Not bad at all. But the pulse count was astronomically high.

I had spotted Suzanne and Annette for what they were. Two free, unfettered dames who could ring bells

7

or have them rung until the cows came home. Though Annette's blood pressure was slightly higher.

Moooooooo!

I called Time. The men on the table looked up at me gratefully. They were pooped, beaten, worn out; and their eyes had that curious dull glaze that suggests they have had enough screwing to last them until Christmas. The young are so stupid, really. College boys. They would learn—eventually. Right then and there, I didn't care.

Suzanne and Annette pushed back from their men and lay back on their haunches. They were a pair of rippling tigresses, all right. I could see the pouts and sulks on their sullen, lovely faces. They were both brunette, tanned and architecturally perfect. And in full bloom. Nineteen, going on toward a million acts of intercourse. I didn't need a crystal ball. I could see it in their futures. Women with asses like they had had changed the history of the world. Ask Caesar, ask Napoleon, ask all the ancient philosophers and sexologists who have seen it happen.

Ask Yankowski, Dillon, Von Firtz—any of the great ones of my field—ask me. I *know*.

I am a leg man, a face man, a breast man, and I do like all that there is that constitutes the female body, but if I had to choose one stimulus, one catalyst that sets the whole thing in motion, I would have to say it was the female ass, hands down. Or *up*.

Suzanne and Annette had two of the outstanding *stimuli* of the world.

For a long quiet moment, the tableau froze. Then as previously indicated, the two naked men rose from the bed, waved to me almost red-faced, as men do, and padded quietly and quickly out of the back door behind the table-bed. The women hadn't moved. They were lying there, gathering their strength, and staring at me. Like two cats in the dark measuring a mouse for a meal.

I smiled at them. They smiled back.

I took off my smock.

They batted their eyes.

I stepped out of my shoes. The ladies squealed with pleasure.

8

They rolled erect, squatting on their rumps, eyeing me up and down. I got down to the buff in record time. When the assets of Rod Damon sprang into view, there was a concerted hoarse intake of breath and one of the women crossed herself.

"Cut that out," I snapped. "I'm a self-made man."

"Mon dieu!" the one on the left giggled, her eyes bulging. "Why did you let me waste my time with that one" —she jerked a shapely shoulder toward the door through which the men had gone—"when you had this treat in store for little Annette!"

"So you're Annette?" I looked at the one on the right, who was now lying back, letting a pink tongue play around her red lips, her eyes doing the seduction routine for me. "Then you are Suzanne?"

"Oui," they chorused.

They were really French. Too good to be true. I remembered now that we always had Exchange Students on tap. What a parlay for me. Two little *mademoiselles* from Gay Paree. I almost said *oolalala!*

"You two sisters by any chance?"

"Oui." Again, they answered in duplicate.

My heart glowed. Siblings! Again a chance to enjoy research while reveling in my favorite form of activity. I really don't need an excuse, but it always warms the cockles of my heart when I can push the culture a step further along the road that Freud got waylaid on. I had tangoed with many a set of sisters in my time. Once there were four sisters in Dayton who had cornered me in a hayloft and one of them had gotten so jealous and upset she nearly impaled herself on a pitchfork. But that's another story. Anyway, I'm always interested in sensational-looking siblings. Far more than I'm interested in being the world's greatest amateur spy; that curious role foisted upon my life by the man I call Walrus-moustache.

That imperious bastard is the one who threatens my sane existence by employing me as a sex-spy-expert in matters best left to the people like the CIA and FBI. But I'm stuck with him. The Thaddeus X. Coxe Foundation gave me the grant that allows me to enjoy my college life. The Coxemen pose as a Far Right group of charitable intent, but in reality they are an undercover ring always

9

interested in keeping the world at peace and free from war. Unhappily, I've had to make like James Bond in the process. Happily, my balls are still intact, no thanks to them. They have put me in the wringer over and over again. I've been lucky enough to stay alive and uncastrated. No thanks to Walrus-moustache who always gives me the most dangerous and sanguine assignments.

"What will you do to us?" Annette cooed, placing both her hands around her own globes to show me how round and willing they were.

"You will be a very naughty boy?" Suzanne suggested, hooking a gorgeous knee in my direction so I could see how deep was down.

"That depends," I said, walking toward them in full-sail. Their hungry eyes followed me, heads going back and forth like spectators at a tennis match. I must admit: The family jewels are incredible to behold even under normal circumstances. Now, they were astounding. I'm the only man who ever drove Nine-Inch Nelson to drink. The man who loved women more than Sex itself. I *inched* past him and he never forgave me for it.

Suzanne and Annette started to gather their muscles, circling me, fanning out, wondering who could get the juiciest morsel first. I held up my hands and clapped them together. They came to attention like the schoolgirls they really were. Their breasts wobbled like Jello.

"All right, girls, listen to me. We are going to try the Sandwich ploy. But there will be no pulling or tugging or fighting or the whole thing is off. Get me?" They nodded their heads rapidly, fearful of dismissal. They looked even yummier as kittens. "Now lie down. Side by side. Just leave enough space for me and mine. Got that?" They did. As quiet as the room was, they were even quieter. Meekly, splendidly, they obeyed me. For a second, I feasted on the two lovely dishes spread out for my sampling and pleasure. There was Annette, on the left again, lying on her back, staring at the ceiling. Long of thigh, limber of leg and bursting of bust. She had a strawberry mole on her left hip. That was a break. I could tell them apart now. And there was Suzanne, holding down the right side of the table. Just as long, lithe and lissome. Their twin navels winked at me. For a mad

10

moment, I wanted to fill things. Then my eyes traveled down. Their Venus mounds, dappled, high-rising, fairly bristled with expectation, in spite of all the energy they had already expended. It made no difference that I could see. The Suzannes and Annettes of this world are always ready. They *stay* ready.

I slid down between them. Easily, lightly, taking great care not to touch them. They moaned and shivered with ecstasy. I lay between them for only a few seconds more. What a pair of bookends they made!

The three of us lay there surveying the ceiling. It needed a paint job. But I'm sure none of us was thinking of that.

The electrodes were off; the charts were still; the lights were low; the anticipation was high. I could tell and they could see it.

"This sandwich—" Annette purred. "How does it go?"

"Yes," Suzanne murmured. "I am so hungry. . . ."

"Patience," I replied. "It is all quite simple. You, Annette, are one slice of bread. You, Suzanne, are the other. I, of course, am the slice of ham, beef or cheese, if you prefer. Now we have all the ingredients, you see, for a fine sandwich. We have only to get down to *making* the sandwich. Understand? It is a love sandwich, but of course."

They giggled, in unison again, but the giggle was charged with fever and unrest and eagerness to get going.

"When do we begin?" Annette begged.

"Yes, when?" Suzanne echoed.

"Now," I said. "I'm hungry too."

They were sisters, all right, each knowing as much about the other as anything short of extrasensory perception allows. In one second flat, we made a sandwich. Annette slammed her slice into me and Suzanne just as quickly pounded her contribution into place. They closed over me like the French finally giving De Gaulle the bum's rush. Only there was love and lollipops in this, not hate and hard times. Annette, lucky for her, was on the front end of the shipping department and in seconds, she was pistoning and pumping for her share of the mayonnaise and salad dressing. I didn't disappoint her.

11

As her eyes widened in surprise, I flooded her. She moaned and cried out in terrified pleasure. Suzanne couldn't wait. In a moment, she had reversed me, vised me with her thighs and she too, responded with a mammoth twitch that accomplished the second coming. It didn't matter. I could go on like that for hours. With the initial fever of the ladies satisfied, we then settled down to the extraordinary niceties and complexities of making a Love Sandwich.

It was a great club job all around.

There was food for all and enough to go around more than once. In no time at all, I had two French converts to the Damon method of Self-Expression. *One* of the methods, that is. I got a million of them.

With rolling eyes, gyrating mounds of flesh, and low whimpers and moans, the sisters devoured me. It was a great arrangement. I couldn't lose for winning. When I was in Annette, Suzanne was behind me, gouging and suckling me. When I was in Suzanne, Annette took over with the extras. Too bad I didn't leave the machines on and the electrodes attached. The room was a symphony of slurps, smacks and collective moans, *oohs* and *aahs* of sexual fun. The sisters had not misunderstood the beauty of the Love Sandwich. While straight intercourse was the main course, there was no end to desserts and *parfaits.* Indeed, the greatest thing about this ploy, which I readily admit is one of my own inventions, is that all three partners wind up thoroughly steamed, reamed and dry-cleaned. There is not a second, or a person, or an area of erogenous zone wasted. The activity, if a bit frenzied and rapid, is at the very least, completely satisfying. No one has ever emerged from the Sandwich ploy sexually unfulfilled.

I felt marvelous. My body was on happy fire, shooting sparks and electricity. And every spark and atom was connected to one of those glorious siblings. They were a better sister act than the Dolly Sisters.

As we drove on toward the explosive climax, wherein the slices of bread completely envelop the meat course, Suzanne and Annette were in the ascendancy. Or rather, Suzanne was above me and Annette below. Suzanne was literally engulfing me with the cheeriest tenderloin of them all. Beneath me, Annette had worked her fingers into a fine tether around my dangling testicles and between these two lovely extremes of womanhood, I was between the devil and the deep blue sea. The room was alive with that humming sound of rare melody; the kind you only hear when the love game is going well. There is no mistaking the sound. It has a joyous rhythm all its own. Later on you realize it's the bedsprings or the table creaking or the meaty slap of warm flesh against warm flesh and then it doesn't matter. You had a ball.

All the way.

Suzanne bit my ear and Annette bit my hip. Between bites, they kept on moving. I pushed for all I was worth. There was a long interval of silent, heaving exaltation. And then I let go again. Red-hot. Both of the girls cried out. I had brought them both home with me. And then the trio of us sank limply, happily, dreamily into a tangled, closed mass of love food. We fused together like molten lava.

The Love Sandwich had been a walloping success.

Nobody was hungry anymore.

Nobody had a mean bone in his body.

It says here.

Annette was sighing, Suzanne was moaning happily and I was nicely closeted with sighers and moaners, when lo and behold, inevitably, the outside world intruded. The one that had Walrus-moustache in it. And bluenoses, prudes, killjoys. And guys who send you on spying missions that have Sudden Death written all over them.

"Really, Damon," Walrus-moustache said grimly, prying the sandwich apart by pulling one of Suzanne's legs one way and one of Annette's another and thrusting his hideously regimental face into my very own, "when, in God's name, do you ever sleep?"

Sleep?

Sleep is for babies, old drunks and juiceless men. I could always sleep. So could he. But the major difference between him and me was that damn Thaddeus X. Coxe Foundation and its peculiar habit of sending spies into the field. He really liked women almost as much.

I closed my eyes and groaned, and Suzanne and Annette began to push their bodies against me insistently,

13

ignoring the tall trim bastard in the bowler hat with a moustache to match.

"Dog!" Annette shouted. "Get out! You interrupt us—"

"Pig!" Suzanne echoed. "Can you not see the professor is occupied?"

"Ladies," I ha-hahed. "We have to humor this man. He has a bad heart and sight of all this joy and good times might make him have a coronary."

Walrus-moustache snorted, not relinquishing his strong hold on the legs of my two slices of bread.

"Damon, please. Do stop for a moment, I beg of you. Then I'll be on my way and you can resume your games. Do tell these charming ladies to take ten—"

"Ten? They'll take all they can get and more—"

But even as he sputtered and fumed, I dug myself out of the nice disorderly pile and got to my feet. Annette and Suzanne cried out in disappointment. But they would have to wait.

Walrus-moustache had returned in all his pompous glory and that meant only one thing.

I was needed as a Coxeman again. To sneak and peek and make love in the name of world peace. A fine job for a man, and generally a ball, but the only trouble was that danger went with the assignment. Very big, very bad danger. The kind of danger that would put my balls on the firing line once again.

"Take it easy," I told the girls as they squatted disgustedly on the bed-table. "Let me talk to this organization man for a few minutes and then we shall continue. He only wants my autograph and another look at a real man."

"Damon." Walrus-moustache's cheeks turned red and purple. His gimlet eyes narrowed. "May you die with an erection. Do stop this nonsense and hear me out." He makes a point of not looking at my best part.

"I'd like to carry you out," I snarled, leading him to the graph and chart machines. Suzanne and Annette lapsed into a low, incomprehensible patois of French whispers and mutters in their corner of the room. "What is it *this* time? The usual? You're sending me to Tim-

14

buktu, I'll bet. Or maybe the Himalayas? I wouldn't be surprised if you wanted me to make a moon shot!"

He lowered his own voice, mindful of the women nearby, and vised my left wrist in a steely hand. He gritted out his next message. The words shot out of him like bullets. And each one of them ruined all my hopes, plans and dreams for the coming days and nights.

"I'd send you to Hell if I could, and stock it with nothing but males, but unfortunately you are needed. Yes, *again*, as you say. Damn you, Damon—something rotten is going on in Czechoslovakia and you are the only operative that can handle it!"

"Of course." I felt the defeat in my throat. I had to go where he wanted me to go. Do what he wanted me to do. You see, way back when my theories and practices were young, I had made carnal use of many an underaged coed to further my research and developments in *Ancient Sexual Customs as Applied to the Modern Woman*. The coeds of course had had the time of their college lives, but legally they were still under the age of consent. Walrus-moustache and/or the Coxe Foundation had been blackmailing me into playing spy with that dodge ever since. Charity, hah! "What seems to be the trouble with the dear old world these days? Nobody getting enough again?"

"Don't joke. We don't know exactly. But our intelligence reports and cumulative data from a small town in Czechoslovakia tells us some strange stories. Here—" Suddenly, he had reached into his dark formal coat and was pushing a thick sheaf of clipped letter-size sheets under my nose. "Read these reports and call me at eleven thirty tonight."

I frowned. That had an ominous sound. "Why at that time?"

"Because," he said icily, "you will be calling from a telephone booth at the airport, and five minutes later you shall be on your way to Switzerland to get more data on the *silver pill*."

"*Silver pill!*" I blurted the words. "I draw the line at tracking down vampires——"

"Hush," he said sternly, jerking a shoulder at Suzanne

15

and Annette who were still pouting in their part of the room. And getting impatient, too. "This has nothing to do with Dracula and you do have your terminology confused. Silver *bullets* felled *werewolves* and this is Czechoslovakia, not Transylvania."

"Big deal. It's all the same to me. I can't even spell Czechoslovakia, and besides, I'm in the middle of research. Myself. Me. I'm needed here. Sexual Response as pertains to——"

Walrus-moustache's frosty smile stilled all my arguments. I saw a lawsuit in each eyeball. Scandal, shame, expulsion from the university. There are so many prudes on faculties, so many killjoys who support a college with grants and monies. Like the Coxe Foundation.

"You'll go. That's certain. You have no choice. I'll leave you now. This shall be our briefest interview. But do, dear Damon, read the reports and call me at eleven thirty. On the dot, you understand. And now I shall wish you luck and take my leave and leave you to your—errr —sexual response research. You are the devil's own, Damon."

"Takes one to know one, you bastard," I said sweetly. "Silver pills! What the hell kind of doubletalk is that?"

"You shall see what you shall see," he said, obliquely and reset his bowler primly on his head. He bowed toward Suzanne and Annette and they fairly spit in his direction, as glad as they were to see him go. He smiled, shrugged, and strode from the room. The bastard was whistling as he left. "The Colonel Bogey March" from *The Bridge Over The River Kwai.* If I'd had a hand grenade I think I would have flung it at his rear end.

As naked as I was, I felt clammy and sticky. Walrus-moustache's assignments always do that to me. Then I shuddered and felt awfully wide open and defenseless. I flung the papers down on the chart table and went back to the girls. I've been very lucky on some dozen jobs for the Coxe Foundation but any one of them could have ended up with me no better off than a capon. You know what this is—a castrated rooster.

Fattened up for the kill—and eating.

"Who was that horrible man?" Suzanne asked, rubbing

16

my thigh. Annette rubbed the other one. I lay back and closed my eyes.

"So grotesque!" Annette agreed.

"He's the man who always has me by the Swanee River. The fly in the ointment, the fifth wheel, the party-pooper. To hell with him. Where were we?"

They showed me.

We repositioned ourselves and I lent it a minor variation. My mind, still gloomily aware of Czechoslovakia and silver pills and unknown trouble beckoning before midnight, returned to the thing that makes me happiest. I speared Annette lustily and allowed Suzanne to dig her spurs into my buttocks. Before we rocked, rolled and ruined each other the only correct way, I had one last thought for them.

"Now—we shall employ a little technique, *cheries?* Five minutes for each side. No more and no less. And then, we shall engage in the *pièce de résistance—soixante-neuf* with *ménage à trois*. Are we agreed?"

They started to *oui, oui* all over the place, so that was settled. And then we really went to town. The French did not invent that glorious number in Sexual Arithmetic known as Sixty-Nine, but the way the Sisters Suzanne and Annette went at it, you could have been forgiven for thinking so. Arab sexology and desert tribes date this routine all the way back to the Nile River, but who cares? Those who know *how, do,* and when it is done properly, very little else in the love world compares to it. So help me, Brigitte Bardot! Gallic *boudoirs* refined the swinging custom to a high art. There's a lot of creativity in it.

Fifty million Frenchmen not only aren't wrong, they are *right*.

So right.

Suzanne and Annette had learned from the experts—the Gods.

I lost sight of them in our concert of kicks and funs. As we pinwheeled and whirled around on the table, each of them nipped and licked with skillful expertise. You couldn't tell their lips apart. They savored each bouncing ball, wrung the last bit of milk from each molten

17

tip I could re-manufacture. Finally, when I was hard enough to drive spikes into the wall, I turned each of them over and whaled away with rare stamina, even for a Damon. Somewhere later, I don't know how much later, I had both their rumps before me and alternated like a guy double-parked in a red light district. I leaped and cavorted, stabbed and lunged à la Flynn as *Robin Hood*. All the arrows in my quiver were put to use. And then my two limp, lovely targets slid off the table in a dead exhausted faint, spilling to the floor in a wild welter of arms, legs and goodies. I didn't say a word to them, and walked over to the machines to reset them. I had more work to do if I wanted to clean up my books before I called Walrus-moustache from the airport. Damn him. He'd given me homework too. The reports I had to read.

I couldn't get Czechoslovakia out of my mind. What could have happened in that staid old burg, besides Communism, to command the services and skills of Rod Damon? I didn't know.

A naked *derrière* on the floor loomed into view again and Annette wobbled to her feet. She was in a daze, but I knew it was her, thanks to the strawberry mole on her left hip.

"*Professeur* . . ." she moaned.

"Yes, Annette?"

"You are . . . a very . . . naughty boy . . . indeed. *Sacre!* . . . they should erect a . . . monument . . . in your honor!"

"I have my own monument," I said.

Her eyes agreed with me. "Never have I seen so formidable an instrument. . . ."

"Lucky. That's me." I fiddled with some dials and knobs on the machine and Suzanne came to life from the other side of the table. She weaved to her feet, her full breasts glowing, her Venus mound in gorgeous disarray. She smiled sleepily across the room at me.

"Marry me," she said simply.

"I would if I could but I can't," I said, not unkindly. "Fact is, I am promised to another—"

"Who?" Annette growled. "Tell us her name and we

18

will cut her heart out!" Suzanne nodded her head so vigorously she gave herself a crick in the neck.

I sighed, eyeing them fondly, soberly thinking of the lost days and nights, lays and delights ahead, no thanks to Walrus-moustache. It *is* a cruel world, my friends. Having to discard two such sisters on such short notice.

"I have to go to Switzerland, my pets. When I come back we shall resume where we left off. It can't be helped, I'm afraid. Duty calls. The ugly man with the garden under his nose has ordered me, and that's it. You· be good until I get back and I'll bring you an Alpine guide, maybe. Or a case of Swiss cheese."

"We will wait," Suzanne and Annette said in chorus, pushing their chests out at me. They licked their lips and their eyes spoke volumes as to how much they would miss me.

Switzerland. And then Czechoslovakia—

Mittel Europa—take it away!

Only it wasn't Switzerland. Or Czechoslovakia. Not right off the bat, at any rate. I suppose Walrus-moustache had lied about the Alp country just to be on the safe side in case Annette and Suzanne overheard his dulcet orders. See what a devious bastard he is?

The way things turned out that night I was on my way to Munich, that famous German city where Adolph made his first big *putsch* in 1933. Just about one hundred miles from the Czechoslovakian border. Well, I'd do some pushing of my own, but that would have to come later. Still, the sonofabitch had booked me on Lufthansa Flight 117 to Munich and at eleven forty-five, right after I was to call him, I would be winging my way across the Atlantic. What fun. What larks.

Besides all that, there was that damn report to read, digest and understand.. More Coxe Foundation hanky-panky. I love the life I lead but not the other side of it— the one where I have to make like Sean Connery and Dean Martin in a spy movie. Movies are all make-believe; the enemies of the Coxe Foundation (and peace-loving mankind) would put even Alfred Hitchcock to shame.

I was so flummoxed and angry with the whole setup that I must have attacked the next ten willing broads who engaged in the sexual-response-blood-pressure ex-

19

periment the rest of that day. I broke them all in savagely, long after their male partners called it quits. But I am always at my best when I behave like Rod Damon, despite my mood. Before I finally packed it in, closing the Study Room, and locking the door until I returned from my travels, if ever, I received five more proposals of marriage, was made the beneficiary of three wills and the other two happy dolls were willing to die with me on a diet of nothing but sex and love.

Now *there* is an experiment worth trying some day.

How long can a man live on nothing but sex?

Even a Rod Damon.

I made a note of it in one of my voluminous notebooks even as I turned over my rolls of graph sheets and charts to the curator of the university library. They would keep them on ice for me until I returned. The university never questions my leaves of absence because Walrus-moustache and the Coxe Foundation arranges them for me well in advance.

The curator is Miss Rawlins, who is one of the few women in the university who is safe from me. And I from her.

Miss Rawlins is almost seventy-five, as bony and skinny as a breadstick and the greatest love of her life was Rudolf Valentino to whom she was forever comparing me and all men to, to our detriment. Miss Rawlins' love affair with a long-dead ghost made it a swell arrangement all around. Her virginity was intact and would remain so until she joined Rudy in that great Movie House In The Sky. She'd never been laid in her life.

But we were pals and as I said goodbye to her, she stared at me almost fondly through her tortoise-shell glasses.

"*Au revoir,* Professor. Do take care. Keep warm. Europe is cold this time of year." Everybody seemed to have the French bug that day.

"Bye, Miss Rawlins. Don't spend all your money on Valentino revivals now. Restrain yourself. Go see a Steve McQueen movie."

She almost blushed. "It's the only way I can ever feel close to him—you know that. Don't tease. Those burn-

20

ing eyes, those lips, that walk he had. He made the tango the most sensual dance in history!"

She could have gone on like that for hours so I pecked her cheek, waved goodbye and *tangoed* out of the library before she could stop me.

If I ever goosed Miss Rawlins, she would have gone through the roof.

Who was I to take her dreams and her Dream Lover away from her?

Maybe she was right.

Maybe Valentino was right.

For all his troubles and his eventual fate, catch him letting the Coxe Foundation send him around the little old world anytime they felt like it! He would have laughed in their faces.

I'm a lover, not a master espionage agent, like I keep telling Walrus-moustache. Who the hell am I to solve the ills of mankind? To make with the guns and the secret devices and the codes and the intrigues when all I ever really wanted out of life was a chance to swing with the nearest available dame?

Dammitall, anyhow—what had happened to the wicked, weary world now that needed the services of Rod Damon, the greatest Coxeman of them all?

Late that night, I found out.

I read Walrus-moustache's report.

All it did was make me feel like throwing up.

The things I had to do for the Coxe Foundation—and world peace at any price.

The Silver Pill Affair was a leftover script from *The Man From U.N.C.L.E.* television show.

That is, it would have been, if there hadn't been a thing called Censorship!

CHAPTER TWO

The Airport was socked in with midnight hues and gusting winds buffeting the control tower but Lufthansa Flight 117 was still getting serviced on the runway with her big shining nose pointing east. By the time I got my flight reservation from the desk and all my luggage checked out, I just had time to make the scheduled phone call to Walrus-moustache. My mood was gloomier than Tax Day. The details of my tall boss's report was a mass of muddled facts, with no definite conclusion. Just guesswork. As educated as it was. I hate leaving town, especially when it has all the earmarks of Le Chase Wild Goose.

The terminal was bursting with nice-looking broads in mini-skirts going in all directions, and a pair of swivel-hipped airline stewardesses made me even more homesick but duty called.

Walrus-moustache's report was another of his masterful exercises in cliche prose and dire prophecy. I had practically memorized the damn thing.

It went something like this:

DAMON:
A foreign power, not yet known to us, has come up with a truly phenomenal gimmick.* You will recall the Russian lady scientist who lessened the virility of the males of the country of Sarmania by liberally dosing the food with a special chemical? You went there and were able to neutralize that situation. Well, now there is a new idea this foreign power has come up with. This country has invented the 'silver pill'. Any man who takes one has the sexual stamina of a young stud—the effects of this pill can make the male potently aggressive for at least five or six hours!
*Had Any Lately? © 1969

I had thought of it and it was ridiculous. So what? If a guy could make the scene for as long as six hours, how the hell could that affect the country or the world? It was progress, real progress, if they asked me. What had that to do with war and bad times? Hard times, maybe, but not the kind that would make any average, healthy, uncomplicated male unhappy!

But Walrus-moustache had his usual boatload of theories and questions. He never lets up.

The report went on:

Now, in the town of Betchnika, population, 10,647, a group of 25 men over the age of 60(!) were given

22

these silver pills. Either by controlled experiment or subversively—you shall have to find out. These elderly gentlemen were so rejuvenated and miraculously aroused that they, in turn, fornicated with their wives, girls on the street, harlots, teenagers and quite truthfully, anything they could get their hands on. (Check also on incident of one of the men with a cow!) Following this curious orgy of plenty, a very curious thing happened. The women of Betchnika began to fight for these men in a jealous rage; and the rest of the men in town began fighting the 25 men who had been ingested with these silver pills. A few days later these 25 men were found hanged in a barn. Yes, hanged! The ghastly affair was hushed up but our Intelligence sources learned of the tragedy through a Red defector we caught in the usual net.

You see how it is? The poor old bastards were having a ball and nobody could leave them alone. What a lousy world it is!

Walrus-moustache's questions nailed down exactly what he and the Thaddeus X. Coxe Foundation wanted to know. But from where I sat all it looked like was that the silver pills were worth having. Look at all the old-timers who'd give their soul for a Fountain of Youth gimmick like that one! A pill that could make you go for six hours—*jinkies!*

1. What were in these pills?
2. Were there any dangerous side effects?
3. For what purpose were they created?
4. Was there a counterdrug, or could the pills be neutralized in any way?
5. If there is a nefarious scheme involved, you are under open orders to use whatever means necessary (including execution) to expedite matters.

I wasn't dense. Open orders, hah. They had the umbrella opened and were asking me to bend over as usual. Just to track down some wonder drug that revitalized the sex glands in some European town in the middle of nowhere. It was all so stupid, really. Medical Science *should* be interested, sure. But why the Coxe Foundation? How in hell could a high-potency aphrodisiac of some kind threaten the world in any way? Except maybe by over-populating that world. Having babies is no crime. Or is it?

I didn't want to have to kill anybody either. With or without sex.

From the telephone booth closest to the entrance gate to Flight 117, I dialed Walrus-moustache's special number at exactly eleven thirty. I had ten minutes in which to do all the complaining I had in me. The terminal was cold and windy, and the black, black night was far from cheering. Especially when I could be back in my private rooms at the university giving more French lessons to Suzanne and Annette. The Coxe Foundation sure knew how to hurt a guy.

The tall trim bastard jumped on the phone after the first ring.

"Ah, Damon. There you are." His slightly English lord-of-the-manor style puts my teeth on edge sometimes. This was one of those times.

"I'd like to strangle you with your old school tie. What the hell is this you're sending me on? This silver pill is a boon, not a menace. You ought to send Schweitzer or Salk——"

"Hush. Don't discuss the project by specifics, if you please. You've read the report?"

"No. I've been out dancing with Elizabeth Taylor. Of course, I read the report. You hear those jet engines in the background? I'm not calling you from some bedroom!"

His chuckle was the four aces kind, as usual. He had me and he knew it. I wasn't kidding him about the engines. They were thundering.

"Good. What do you think of the report?"

"Just what I said. What's the threat? Who's worried? How does it get anybody in trouble?"

"Damon, Damon. Twenty-five senior citizens were murdered. Hanged. Doesn't that suggest foul play?"

"Sure does. The old guys acted like roosters, and as happens to roosters the world over, they got hung up."

"Precisely. But we'd be fools to think jealousy was the outstanding motive. At any rate, we must investigate this.

24

If the—ah—pill is a certitude, then we must command its use, at any cost. Don't you see what a weapon it could be in the wrong hands?"

"Killjoy. So what if the kids got hold of it—you were young once too, you know."

"I am not speaking of kids or children or teenagers. I speak of the hostile powers. Sex, as you know, is still the greatest secret weapon in the world. Who knows how they could use it to their benefit? That I should have to tell *you* this, of all people—"

"Yeah, but it's no secret with me." I looked at my watch. Five minutes had sped by. "Okay, okay. So I go to Munich. To do what?"

His tone became brisk. He likes dishing out instructions. Some guys have that hang-up. And he has, in spades.

"Good man. Your first set of directions are simple. You will receive further instructions in relays, as you go along. Now, you will arrive in Munich tomorrow and go to a place known as *The King's Inn*. It's rather an old meeting-place tavern where the locals gather to eat and drink their Bavarian beer. There you will meet another agent, one Christina Ketch. A very beautiful woman, which should be to your tastes. She is five-foot-nine, flaxen-haired, very fair-skinned and quite authoritative, they tell me. You'll have no trouble spotting her. Make connections with her. You will both remain in the inn until you are contacted. Is that clear?"

"It's a long way to go just to meet a blonde. Okay. Any code? Password? How will she know me?"

He chuckled again.

"You do manage to think like an agent for a time, don't you? Very good. When you see her, simply walk up to her and say—and this I confess is my own notion—*'What's a nice girl like you doing in a Bavarian joint like this?'* Those must be the exact words, you see. Not a preposition or noun off. And she will answer, again without any deviation from the letter of the reply—*'Waiting for lightning to hit my rod!'* There, what do you think of that?"

"Brilliant. You ought to write material for the Joey Bishop Show."

"Thought you'd like it. Now, get going. You've got just about five minutes to catch that plane. A pleasant flight, my dear Damon."

"Up yours, Walrus-moustache."

"Certainly. *Ta.*" I never offended him, not while he was winning. After all, he wasn't the one who had to fly to Europe in the dead of night.

Controlling my temper, I flung out of the phone booth, dodged a fat female in furs fiddling with a big, black pocketbook and headed out to the waiting plane. It looked like a big silver arrow in the lights of the runway. Silver. *Aggrrrhhh.* All that did was remind me of my mission and I wasn't kindly disposed toward Silver that night. I think I would have kicked the Lone Ranger's horse in the ass if he had come pounding across the field in a cloud of dust with the speed of light.

And then I saw the stewardess on the airstair of Flight 117 and the world turned over on its back and lay down. *Va-va-voom* and *ring-a-ding-ding!* Munich flights had their rewards after all.

I practically galloped up the airstair and made sure I collided with her as she came forward to greet me. There was a line of passengers flowing up the stair, but I didn't let that bother me.

"Welcome to Lufthansa," she said in the usual, cheery greeting that was spaded out for all comers, but by that time I had missed her smile and deftly bumped into her body. I didn't lay a glove on her but she couldn't have missed the solid presence of one Rod Damon. She didn't. The creamiest skin this side of vanilla ice cream flushed and she tried to smile as she re-righted her sky cap atop her lovely head. She was a medium-sized, but staggeringly endowed young woman, and not even the blue pert uniform could hide the finely feminine lines they contained.

"'Scuse me," I said. "I get dizzy on stairs."

"That's quite all right, sir—" she stammered. She was stammering because she couldn't believe I was not carrying a cane or baseball bat or something. Anything that could have caused that very definite *lump* she had felt. I brushed by her and that opportunity afforded one more passage of arms. Again, she recoiled, she blushed and

26

her eyes followed me as I went down the thickly carpeted aisle toward my seat at the rear of the plane. I was smiling to myself because I knew I had her. I had to have. She was about twenty by 36X24X36 and how much could she have lived in such a short time? *Coffee, Tea or Me?* is a hoax.

So I sat in my comfortable rear window chair, watched the lights of the field, waited for the roar of the engines and lapsed into a nice tranquil frame of mind. Luck was on my side too. The seat next to me was vacant. And nobody showed up to take it. I forgot all about Munich and silver pills and let the jet rock me into a state of euphoria. It always feels great when you know there is a great-looking, very curious broad in your immediate vicinity. Curiosity doesn't only kill cats; it draws virgins like flies. There are things about men they just have to find out for themselves.

We were airborne in no time at all. I forgot all about the other passengers too. The old people who needed pillows and comforters; the yawning, frightened folk taking maybe their very first flight; and all the seasoned veterans who were already too drunk to notice much. Lots of people drink their flight nerves away in the airport bar hours before flight time. It was a quiet bunch all around. Especially since it was almost midnight and most of the good S.O.B.'s were already trying to catch some shut-eye. Somebody was already snoring.

The lights of the city below were behind us in no time at all. Space and the inky blue sky beckoned. Flight 117 roared on toward the ocean. And the Atlantic. And Munich. And God knows what else.

I waited only about an hour. The plane droned on, peacefully, no turbulence, no talking. All was quiet on the airline front. I lay back in my chair in the window seat and closed my eyes. She'd come, all right, or I didn't know anything about women. Or virgins, that very rare breed.

When I heard her drop lightly into the seat next to me, I also felt her sturdy leg brush against my ankle. It was warm and vibrant, that leg.

"Sorry," she murmured. "Mind if I catch a smoke back here? This seat's empty—"

27

"Be my guest."

I opened my eyes and looked at her. Her profile was splendid. A turned-up nose, hollow cheeks and a fine chin. The rest of her profile was sheer whistle-stuff. I leaned toward her and made myself more comfortable. I took her hand and she shivered slightly but she didn't try to take it away. After all, the rear of the cabin was dark and the couple directly across the aisle, a middle-aged married team, were fast, fast asleep.

Her glowing cigarette tip lit up her face. She was heavenly-looking, even if the figure was hellish.

"Wilhelmina is my name," she said softly.

"I'm Rod," I said. I played with her fingers. She let me. Even when I strayed them toward my lap, she didn't flinch. She was finally getting exactly what she came for. But she was trembling just the same.

"What kind of work are you in?" Now I could hear the barest traces of German accent. A Rhineland maiden, all right, even if the name wasn't proof positive.

"I'm a houseboy at a dice table," I said.

She was as green as a salad. "Really? What kind of work is that?"

"Child's play. Tell me about yourself, Wilhelmina. You look so young and pretty and young and pretty—"

She laughed and began to tamp the cigarette out in her seat ashtray. She had to swivel her body to do that. Her beam was so good I wanted to run my hands all over it. But I restrained myself. I couldn't give her the excuse to fly until she had gotten her hands on what she had come to find out. Was aching to find out.

With the cigarette extinguished, she turned to me again and I took the bull by the horns. I took her hands and placed them across my crotch. Her sharp hiss of breath should have wakened the whole sleeping plane but it didn't. She inclined toward me and our faces were inches apart. I kissed the tip of her nose.

"I don't believe it," she whispered.

"Seeing is believing. Touching is. Be my guest."

"You're sure you don't mind? It's just that how often does—"

She stopped herself, shaking her head, but I didn't give her time to renege. In two seconds flat, I unsheathed and the miracle popped into view, snaking through her fingers. Again she almost blurted, but this time, she very wisely trapped it in her hands and held it. Her palms were cool, her fingers soothing. I sat back and smiled. I felt marvelous. Reborn, as it were. *Without silver pills.*

"Talk to me," I said.

"I don't want to talk—Rod. It's amazing how big things look from up here, isn't it?"

"Ain't it the truth?"

"Like you could reach down and touch it with your hand. And stroke it. And hold it and squeeze it. Airplane travel is the end-all, isn't it?"

"It sure is."

"You know something—if I could take a cloud in my hand I'd like nothing better than to fluff it, pat it and make a pillow for my head."

"Hey. You're a poet. Poetess. You know that?"

She was also very smart. Virgin or not. She was speaking at a conversational level all the time while her magical hands had their play with me. I was beginning to feel the pressure. I grew and grew, swelling and ballooning, and Wilhelmina was becoming goggle-eyed with disbelief and wonder. The time had come.

"Wilhelmina, I'm cold. Could you fetch a blanket?"

"Certainly. Back in a minute—" She broke all the records getting out of her seat and tripping down the aisle. Even before I could rearrange my chair to a full reclining position she was back. Breathless. Eyes shining in the dark. The family jewels do it every time.

She plumped the comforter over me, hiding me from the world at large, rambling on about St. Moritz being lovely this time of year and how much she liked to take a week's vacation skiing in the Alps. By that time, she had squirmed down beside me, still staring straight ahead, but under the blanket, her hips had done an amazing swivel to the left, facing me and we were off to the races. Further conversation was not necessary. Virgins these days are very smart. While she had gone off to fetch the blanket, she had also gotten rid of her panties and bra. Instinctively, she knew all the right moves. Or I had underestimated her badly. But I still didn't think so.

Her time had merely come, that was all, and Damon brings out the best in everybody.

She came around with her hips, and suddenly under the blanket, the creamiest, softest thighs in all creation had parted to meet Noah's Ark. I slipped in, guided not only by my native experience but by her trained, cooling hands. She was a virgin, all right but she was eager, excited and willing to be hurt a little to get a lot. She started lubricating like mad as soon as I found the glory hole, and after that, we settled into a nice, smooth orgiastic dance of hips, knees, thighs and navels. She was fragrant, clean and delicious. The blanket began to bob like a big cork on the waves. The Yankowski ploy was made for forty-five degree angles.

"Rod—do you often fly like this?"

"Every time I get the chance."

"God, how wonderful!"

"You like flying, Wilhelmina?"

"It's marvelous!"

"It has its points," I agreed.

She sighed dreamily as a shaft of light, gold and pure moonbeams, inundated her. She twitched gratefully and then she rammed her pelvis at me with one long fervent thrust. I met it and we held the moment for a full ten seconds before she moaned as quietly as a kitten and sank down into her seat. Her skycap was askew, her blonde hair was awry and her airstair was thoroughly renovated. Victory Through Air Power was mine once again. Yankowski's Method of Angular Attack!

And once more the hours, the miles of flight had swept by incredibly fast. Unnoticed and unboringly happy. And busy.

Suddenly she was sobbing. Soft and low. Frowning, because she might wake up my sleeping fellow passengers, I huddled her in my arms. She wept on, sniffing now, crying like a teenybopper who missed a pot party.

"Willie, what's the matter?"

"It's nothing," she whimpered. "I'll be all right. It's just that I knew my first time would be in the sky. I knew it would happen that way. It was meant to be. And now that it has happened—I'm so *happppppy!*"

That brought on a fresh deluge of tears. A Niagara.

I had to shut her up. Somehow. I did, the only way I knew how. I drew her toward me, found the airstair and made another three-point landing. Tip and ball contact. She stopped crying. She vibrated like a tuning fork and hummed.

She was really happy then. So happy, she bounced up and down like a kid with a new toy. Well, it was. The Damon Joy Toy. It's made so many people happy. Girl-people, I mean. I'm no queer.

So Wilhelmina enjoyed herself and so did I and Flight 117 raced on toward Munich. I lost track of what time it was when she finally crept back to her job serving coffee and sandwiches at dawn and generally making do for the S.O.B.'s. She had done fine for me.

Believe me, it's the only way to run an airline.

And the *only* way to fly.

CHAPTER THREE

Flight 117 touched down in Munich, Wilhelmina kissed me a tearful farewell and put her breasts into it, and I promised devoutly I'd look her up on the flight back. Maybe even take her to St. Moritz for skiing and sheing. Both propositions tickled her and she jiggled nicely in appreciation. But tearstained airline stewardesses, no matter how well constructed, were far from my mind once the plane landed. The prospects of *The King's Inn* and meeting my new blonde contact, Walrus-moustache's fair-skinned, flaxen-haired female, were running around in my head. That and the mystery of silver pills and Betchnika lynchings. If the Coxe Foundation had to know why twenty-five men over sixty were hanged because they were oversexed, then I had to find out too. After all, it was Sexology research, also. And that is the name of my game.

But Wilhelmina got a stranglehold on me and mine between the customs counter and the airport terminal door leading out. She just wrapped her goodies around me, kissed me lustily, and churned her pelvic cage into mine. Shameless hussy!

"Darling," she murmured. "You *must* come back."

31

"I always do. Like a bad penny."

"You are the greatest man I ever met."

" 'Twas ever thus."

"Never have I known flying to be such a trip! You're better than all the LSD in the world."

"True, true. Well, Willie, *auf wiedersehen,* so long, goodbye, and meet you in the wild blue yonder someday. Soon."

That was when she started to cry, and hug and squeeze and her fine hands attacked the family jewels again. Right out there in the open, in front of all those people getting their luggage checked for entry into Germany. She just didn't give a damn for appearances.

"Willie, please—"

"But I may never see you again! Never know the touch of you, the *feel* of you—" She demonstrated and I had to pull myself loose. Her tears were staining my nice suit.

"Them's the breaks, kid. Be a big girl now. Damon will return. I promise you." She'd practically put the grapes through a wringer.

"Oh, if only I didn't have to fly on to Budapest. Rod, Rod—kiss me, *liebchen* and be a good boy in *München.*"

"I eat all over," I grinned. Munich. *München.* What an opening.

"Beast." She slapped me lightly and we kissed, putting everything we had left into it. Willie groaned aloud at her loss. My virginial skycap would never be the same again. I had made a woman of her and she knew it. She wasn't going to wait twenty more years for sex.

My last sight of her was going away. Me out the door, her toward the powder room on the next level, above the escalator stairs. She walked tall and proud even though her shoulders in the blue uniform were shaking with sobs. She had a rear end like the first horse in a parade. Sighing, I tightened my grip on my bag and attaché case and went out the revolving glass doors to the sidewalk to look for a cab. And get a good look at Munich. Hitler's old backyard.

The educated ghosts of Dealey, Yankowski, De Loma and Von Firtz, as well as that horny old Arab, Jalal al-Din al-Siyuti, cursed at me in five languages for deserting the virgin I had introduced to the field of battle. All these sexologists, centuries apart but closer than the pages of a book in womanizing, had all agreed that of all women to instruct in love-play and erotica, the endowed virgin reigns supreme. They can give you prime time and superior cooperation because of their willingness to learn. And the freshness of their skin and flesh.

"*Tophole!*" as Dealey would say.

"*Da!*" Yankowski once said. "*Never a nyet will they say!*"

"*Madonna!*" was De Loma's contribution, and that wily Teuton, Von Firtz, simply called a virginal encounter a "*Gott in himmel!*" As for my Arab mentor, whom I idealized above all others—his word was law to me— he is untranslatable, really, but it would boil down to something like "*Yeah, Bo!*"

But duty called. I had to get to *The King's Inn* and check out the action. Especially if Christina Ketch was waiting for me.

I looked at Munich.

It looked at me.

I was too young for World War II but I remembered all the war movies, the history books and newsreels. It looked just fine for a city that had been marched through by the tanks and men of the Seventh Army. Whatever bombing there had been had all practically disappeared. You couldn't tell for looking. Munich is about as cosmopolitan as, say, Manhattan, New York, or Chicago, Illinois. There are big stone buildings, fine boulevards, a populace always on the go, and nothing about the dress and manner of the civilians could make you think you were in Germany until you started reading street signs and shop windows. Otherwise, you see just as many Volkswagens as you do in the good old U.S.A. Just as noisy and hectic a burg as anyplace Stateside. It figured. The Yankee Dollar had come to Munich in a floodtide right after the event called V-J Day. And the Marshall Plan and Big Business and let's-forget-that-lousy-war-and-the-man-called-Adolph had done the rest. You can't see any crematoria stacks anymore. Even though Dachau is a stone's throw away.

A cab found me, swallowed me up, and I gave the

driver the address of *The King's Inn*. He looked at me a moment, shrugged, and then batted his meter gadget. His face was worn and creased like a beat-up wallet.

"Why the face, Fritz?"

We ploughed out into traffic and his vehicle, a Ford design made up to seem European, meshed with a flow of cars heading East.

"I am Wilhelm," he said, stiffly. It was my time for Willies. "Do you go to *The King's Inn* to try the Bavarian beer and wines or did you simply want a drink? It is rather early in the day, *mein Herr*, for an interesting time at *The King's Inn*." His voice was reedy, frog-filled.

He had spotted me for a tourist and it was early. It wasn't very late in the afternoon, Munich time. The day was gray, smoky. Cool.

"They rent rooms, don't they?"

"That too. In which case, any time is proper."

He was a thin, withered, old-timer. The kind who might have worn a swastika before I was born. His hoarse throat could be from too many *Sieg Heils!*

"How far is it?"

"Not very far. Perhaps ten kilometers—fifteen minutes."

I sat back on the leather seat, folded my arms, and watched the sweeping panorama of buildings, store fronts, cobbled alleys, going by. We were rapidly entering a more Teutonic-seeming section of the city. I spotted signs on hanging stanchions, curtained bakery windows, even a stable or two leading right out into the thoroughfare. The tavern signs were beginning to show up more frequently. Beer is where the German is. Without his stein, a Rhinelander is naked.

"*Amerikaner?*" Wilhelm said, idly enough. But his eyes in the rearview mirror were tired, amused. I kept my cool. Walrus-moustache had taught me to be wary of any strangers and newcomers when I was in the field working as a Coxeman. Some of his instructions had rubbed off.

"Want to see my tattoo? I have the first stanza of 'The Star-Spangled Banner' printed right across my ass."

That made him smile a bit more warmly and then I

figured he was a harmless hackie. Same breed of weary travelers from Siam to Brooklyn.

"*Mein Herr* has a sense of humor. *Gut*. There is very little to laugh about in Germany these last twenty-five years."

I nodded, feeling better. At least we agreed about that.

"Where's that beer hall where Hitler made his first push in '33?"

He jerked a contemptible thumb. "Far over. Other side of town. It is nothing. You wouldn't care to see it."

"I agree. How's the women in Munich?"

He grinned wryly. "You have two choices. Streetwalkers or grandmothers. And many, many a widow."

"Real gay town, huh?"

"A cemetery in my opinion." Wilhelm spun the cab around a corner, found a narrow, cobbled lane and then sped out into another main artery of traffic. I saw a sign that said, KING'S INN OSTEN. "Not too far now. We have made good time for a Friday."

"Suits me. I need a shower, a hot meal. The works. And I also want to sample this famous Bavarian beer I've heard tell about."

"And what kind of employment is *mein Herr* in?"

Everybody wanted to know my business. I played it dumb. And for laughs, strictly. Besides, you never could tell.

"I'm a contraceptive salesman. You know—prophylactics. Rubbers."

"Oh." His hoarse voice was a low nothing sound.

"What kind do you use? *Sheiks, Trojans, Four X?* I hope none of them because I represent *Thinnies*. New line. And business is expanding. Ballooning, you might say."

Wilhelm muttered under his breath.

I tapped his shoulder. "You were saying—?"

He shrugged, trapped. "I am sixty-seven, *mein Herr*. I have not been good for a woman since I had my triple hernia. It is just as well. With the prices of things as they are, I could not afford a woman. Any woman. Also, I have not had that drive for a woman that a man must have. Not in years. Not since my Bertha died. In '49."

I kept my face serious. And gambled. "Really? Too

35

bad. It's a shame. You ever take a silver pill? It's on the market now. A super-drug. It revives a man and makes him capable of remaining *active* for a good six hours."

Wilhelm had to slam on the brakes to avoid running up the back of a Volkswagen. When he straightened himself out, his face twisted toward me as he played with the steering wheel. His old eyes had taken on a hopeful glow. He looked almost *hopefully* insane.

"*Mein Herr* is amusing himself with Wilhelm—"

"Scout's honor. Ask anybody. Ask your old cronies."

"But it is not true. We have never heard of such a thing. And I'm not ashamed to say we all have tried everything. Bee's cream, patent drugs, glandular shots from our doctors—silver pills? If only it were true—where could one get his hands on such a treasure?"

"It is new," I admitted, "but Munich being so up-to-date and all, I was sure you'd have it here. Well, just ask your local druggist. Or your doctor."

Wilhelm's voice rose, the frogs evicted. But I had found out what I wanted to know. He didn't know about silver pills and the mass execution in Betchnika. Or the old roistering joy boys who had had a ball before they died. The calamity had not leaked across the Czech frontier.

"That I shall do. And I am grateful to you, *mein Herr. Gott!* To think I could get my hands on that fat-assed waitress who always laughs at me in *Muller's!* She would see what a man Wilhelm was when he was in his prime!"

"That's the spirit."

"I would make her cry and beg for more and then I would turn her over on her stomach and do it again!"

"Go get her, Wilhelm."

There were tears in his eyes, too. Who said Germans weren't emotional? Between this old cabdriver and the young skycap, I could have filled the Rhine.

I felt lousy about lying to the old rat, but what's wrong with hope? Even if it was a dream, his mind would be filled with glorious pictures of conquest until he found out that there wasn't anything on the open market like I had said. But who knows? He might firm up just *thinking* there was. Stranger things have happened. Remember—even Casey must have got another time at bat in baseball heaven.

Suddenly the terrain changed.

The buildings vanished, the lane opened into country. I began to see a cow or two, and trees, trees, trees. Now, the mighty height of the Bavarian Alps, snow-capped and magnificent, crowded the horizon to the east. As gray as the day was, the majesty of those peaks was awesome. We haven't got anything like it back in America, really, and I am including the Rockies and the Sierra Nevada. Also, I began to spy a dairymaid or two or three. From the moving cab, they all looked like Ingrid Bergman in the good old days of *For Whom The Bell Tolls* and *Spellbound*.

Long rows of towering spruces and elms lined the roadway, and Wilhelm piloted the machine happily, his mind filled with the prospects and pleasures of the silver pills. Like a mental orgy with bells on.

I was beginning to enjoy the view, like any hick or traveling salesman, when Wilhelm slammed on the brakes. We lurched to a stop in a pleasant little bower of flowers and ivy with the background of trees and mountains making the whole tiny area as picturesque as any post card. There was a sense of peace and beauty and the idea of being a spy and going to investigate a clan-type lynching seemed as remote as a wart on Raquel Welch's fanny. Who would think such a thing?

"The King's Inn," Wilhelm said triumphantly, and cranked his meter flag. "We are here."

"How much do I owe you?"

Wilhelm spread his hands. "If you have American money I should like to have it. Say the sum of three dollars. But no tip, mind you. I am grateful to you for what you have told me. If it is true, it is worth a million tips!"

"But, Wilhelm—"

"No, no. I insist. My pleasure."

"You're sure? Money goes a long way, you know—"

"Please, *mein Herr*. I will be happy with three American dollars. As a memento of our discussion. I would not use it even to buy my first silver pill!"

So I paid him the three dollars, not having converted

37

all my money to marks yet. One thing about the Coxe Foundation; they give you plenty of expense money to do their dirty little jobs. Real clean money.

Wilhelm saluted me like a Prussian officer, wheeled his cab around and drove out of my life, forever. I thought forever anyway. I wouldn't want to run into him again when he found out that the silver pill was a secret invention that nobody knew anything about. Including *Amerikaner* me. The fink.

The King's Inn was a fraud.

It seemed no more than a gabled, shuttered, gingerbread house with a pebbled pathway leading up to a front door that resembled the entrance to a barn. You know the type. The door split in half that opens from the top or bottom or both. There was a sign shaped like a beer mug, lettered in Gothic figures that made the name of the place almost unreadable because of the crowding of the symbols. But it was Old World, for all of that. I expected to see good, pink-faced *burgers* with their *Meerschaums* and tankards of ale and kneepants with Tyrolean hats. The works. But like Wilhelm had said, it was too early in the day; there wasn't a vehicle in sight. Not a car or a cart or a hayrick. There *was* a fine, heavy aroma of wine and cheese, though. The fragrance wasn't exactly perfume, but to a wine-drinker I imagined it could be ambrosia and nectar. I'm a fan of Old Charter bourbon myself, but what the hell. You drink what you like and I'll drink what I like.

A bird chirped in a nearby tree and I palmed some sweat off the tip of my nose. The day was sunless but it was warm. There wasn't even a country breeze to cool me off. I stalked to the front door of *The King's Inn,* toting my bag and attaché case. I was a little pooped, but mainly physically uncomfortable. I needed a bath or a shower or both. And some bacon and eggs, or knockwurst and sauerkraut. Whatever. I wouldn't be choosy.

I knocked on the closed door of the inn. There was no knocker or bell or anything. Just stout oaken boards side by side, studded with brass-headed nails. The wood was brown and clean. As if a recent rain had washed it bare.

There was no answer.

Again I knocked.

Silence.

The bird stopped chirping and buzzed off, frightened. I set both bags down and drew back to really batter the panel. Just at that moment, the top half shot back and I was looking into a pair of bold blue eyes blinking out at me from the gloom of the unlighted interior of the place. Below the eyes was a pug nose, a red wide mouth with thick lips and then a defiant chin. From that point down, the view flowered into two of the largest mammary illusions (or realities) ever visited upon womankind. The boobs were incredible; the waist beneath it tinier than Twiggy's. That was all I could see. The lower half of the front door, closed, shut out everything else.

"So?" The girl, who looked all of eighteen, shrilled. "Who comes?"

"Who else?" I smiled and doffed my hat.

She leaned out, frowning, resting both arms on the top of the low part of the door. A thin shelf of wood accommodated her arms. They were pink like the rest of her, baby fat rolling. The face wrinkled in a scowl, completely unfeminine, having nothing to do with my looks or my words.

"You want something?" she barked. "What is?"

"This is an inn, isn't it? I'd like a room, something to eat. And to drink. And a smile if you can spare one." The girl snorted.

"How long you stay? One night? Two? Three?" She held up three pudgy fingers. "You take room for week? Got festival of wine coming up. Can't bother with fly-by-nighters."

"Let me in," I sighed. "And we'll talk it over. I flew by night and now it's daytime. I also have money. Lots of money. And if you're a good little girl I'll let you have a look at it. Are you the innkeeper?"

She laughed. "No. Gretchen. Landlord's daughter. You come. We see. Carry own luggage, please. It's time to milk the cows and no get fresh milk if hands dirty. Come, please."

She swung open the bottom half of the door and the rest of her tapered down to cream and butter and delectability. When the baby fat left, she would be a destroyer supreme. Right now, she was fleshed out mightily. When she turned around to lead me into the inn proper, the skirt and apron she wore seemed to be keeping her two mountainous buttocks tied into place. Captive balloons, all the way.

Gretchen.

The landlord's daughter.

Talk about traveling salesmen. I was beginning to feel like one all over. I wondered if there was only one extra bed and would I have to sleep with Gretchen in that one. You don't know farmers and country fathers. They'll do anything to unload a spinster daughter. Anything. Though there wasn't a blessed thing wrong with Gretchen that losing ten pounds wouldn't cure. Plus her whine and her snarls and frowns. Poor kid. Probably never been properly laid. It happens to a lot of daughters the world over, and they go into womanhood shrilling liks nags and shrews. Well, we'd see about that.

"Name, please?" she asked over her shoulder as she went around a registration desk of sorts that was no more than a cubicle in the dim hallway. The wallpaper was atrocious. Knights, heralds, spears, lances, and deer rampant against a field of clovers. Everybody was hoisting one.

"Rod Damon. I'm from America."

Me and my big mouth.

She dropped the pen she had picked up, turned white, and then she screamed. And fainted. I couldn't catch her. She fell like a ton of bricks behind the counter. With all the crashing roar of a brick shithouse.

It all happened so fast I stood there with egg on my face and the scream lingering in my ears. She sounded exactly as if she had been raped. Or wanted to be. I couldn't figure out which.

Little did I know, to coin a nifty original.

My fame, as sometimes happens, had preceded me.

Even as I raced around the counter to make sure she was all right, I could see the half-opened book lying on the counter of the cubicle. A quick glance was all I needed and then I was bending over Gretchen and picking her up and carrying her to a nearby chair. I had

40

to resist the urge to pull her up to a standing position via her tremendous whim-whams, they were such superb handholds. This kid was *built*.

The book?

Nothing but the Damon classic, in its ninety-fifth printing since 1968, *ONLY A MAN CAN DO IT FOR YOU*, or *THREE HUNDRED WAYS TO LOVE A WOMAN*. This copy was so dog-eared, thumb-stained and grease-lined, Gretchen must have read it a dozen times. Before, during and after milking cows.

It figured.

Another virgin had crossed my path and the trail toward the mystery of the silver pills was being literally strewn with them. Maybe it was a trend. How did I know Gretchen was a virgin?

Don't be silly.

Who else but a virgin would pass out before a guy even laid a finger on her?

Only a virgin would be green enough to do that and miss all the first fun.

CHAPTER FOUR

Later on I got a nice back room upstairs, at the end of the second floor, which was the top one, and it commanded a fine view of the hills and dales and mountains. I also got a hot meal of green pea soup, knockwurst and sauerkraut and all the coffee I could drink. Then a large wooden tub was placed at my disposal plus a thick bar of yellow laundry soap and several woolly towels. I began to feel a lot better.

But none of this came to pass until I got Gretchen revived and the landlord came running to see what all the screaming and commotion was about. Landlord, hah. It was Gretchen's mother and she was everything her daughter was with about forty pounds extra. Still, as the Italian sexologist, Giuseppe Gorgonzitti said, *"What nature has not forgotten, will give you much to remember!"* You know how Italians are. They like everything in abundance. Loren, Vesuvius, babies, etc. Gretchen's mamma would have made old Gorgonzitti do a *tarantella* of lust.

She was big, beefy, clean-skinned and mammoth. Quite an armful in any league. And when she saw me slapping poor Gretchen awake, she near clapped her hands with joy. I got the picture the first time. Mamma was dying to unload Gretchen. Even though she probably made the kid do all the work, including being barmaid as well as dairymaid. I sensed the absence of a stern Pappa.

When Gretchen came to, batting her wide eyes in amazement that the great Damon was actually a guest at her mother's inn, Mamma hushed her and sent her off to milk some cows. The old girl—not old really; she couldn't have been more than thirty-nine on a clear day —winked at me to be silent until Gretchen left. Flushed and trembling, Gretchen stumbled out, clutching her copy of *ONLY A MAN CAN DO IT FOR YOU*. She'd been too dazed to even ask for an autograph, but that could wait. Mamma was studying me from top to bottom, even as she took my money and signed me in. But she had more than dollar signs in her eyes.

"I am Mamma. You will call me Marlene. Like Dietrich. So, you are he. The great one who has my daughter in circles. Why do you come here to Munich?"

Now I winked. "An affair of the heart, *mein Frau*. I am to meet a lady here tonight. When you serve the wines and beers."

She chuckled and jabbed a heavy thumb into my ribs. Her breasts rolled and so did her eyes. She had a red, wanton mouth.

"I am no madam, my American. Remember that. I am glad you are here, though. Tell me. Do you like my little Gretchen?"

"She's peachy," I said.

"Is she not? Very lovely, very smart. But she is a prisoner here. Her head full of ideas, full of faraway places like America. And men. She is yet a virgin. Think of that. Why, at eighteen I had already had my pick of a dozen of the men from the village. But my Gretchen? *Ach!* She will let no one near her. I am doomed to watch out for her best interests."

"I'd like a bath," I said. "And some food. The plane

42

trip was a bore. I must change my clothes."

She wouldn't let me change the subject.

"You will get those. And more. Listen to me, Herr Damon. I am no bluenose. If Gretchen catches your fancy, well—you are a man. A famous one, to hear her tell it. Well, follow your own conscience. I will not interfere. My daughter is taken with you already. As if that book of yours had not done enough!"

I shrugged. "Did you read the book?"

She wagged her head. "A page or two. But you can tell me and show me nothing I do not already know."

"You'd be surprised."

Mamma Marlene smiled. She chuckled. She giggled. And then she gave me another jovial poke in the ribs that nearly dislocated several vertebrae. She was as aggressive as a lady wrestler.

"Would I? Perhaps. We shall see. In any case, welcome to *The King's Inn*. You are welcome here and you will like the beds. Genuine eiderdown."

She wasn't kidding me. She expected me to nail Gretchen at the first opportunity and then play the outraged mother demanding I do the right thing.

So that's how I got my room.

There seemed to be no men about the place. Just Gretchen and Mamma. What a setup. Later that night, some bartenders and waiters would show up, but in the meantime, in between-time, if I had the notion, I could have a lot of fun. Marlene Zimmer and her Gretchen liked me.

So I ate a good meal.

So I bathed. In the big wooden tub with the gallons of hot water fetched in by Gretchen. Then she tiptoed out meekly and I undressed and got down to the buff, drinking coffee and feeling wonderful.

The afternoon wore on and I drowsed in the nice hot tub. There was a scent of lilacs in the air from the open windows. The curtains fluttered. The air had turned balmy. I felt lethargic and pleasantly lifeless. You know the feeling. Not a care in the world. Oh, yeah.

I don't know when it was but just as I was about to step out of the big wooden tub, Gretchen tiptoed back into the room. She closed the door softly and shot the

43

bolt home so that it wouldn't squeal on her. I watched her with some amusement. The poor kid was still dressed in her peasant blouse, skirt and apron, and her face was tired but her eyes were doing flip-flops of curiosity and anticipation. She drew closer to the tub and I lay back, knees jutting upward. She halted at the rim of the vat and stared down at me. Her tremendous chest of treasures was going up and down like an elevator. The tiny waistline was still ridiculous.

"Oh," she said.

"Yes?" I said.

"It's . . . so . . . *big!*"

"Uh huh."

"And . . . it . . . *floats!*" She didn't mean the laundry soap.

"Of course it does. It is the most buoyant part of a man's body."

"Could I . . . just . . . touch it?"

"I'd like that."

She got down on her knees, her breasts straining against the low-cut peasant blouse and her right hand reached out exploratively. I had some fun with her, making her target jump and twitch a little. The thing eluded her at first and the unpretty scowl started to come back into her creamy face, but when she finally trapped it, her face warmed up like toast.

"Oh, oh," she marveled. "Both hands I need!"

"So? Who's stopping you?"

"Almost insanely, she grabbed the family jewels with both hands and for a second, she must have felt the same sensation she had with one of her cows. She began to hand-pedal me, up and down. And all that did was make the miracle larger. Her eyes popped.

"*Donnerwetter!*" she blurted. "You are getting *larger—*"

"A natural reaction with the healthy male, my dear Gretchen. Try Vixen and Prancer and Blitzen and see what happens—"

She was beyond hearing me. She had guided me to her face and placed her warm cheek alongside. She crooned. She hummed. She moaned, and her nice strong fingers played and played. Before I could stop her or

44

wanted to, she was raining kisses on the prize. It was a great finish to the act of bathing. I was transported. The kid had possibilities.

"Gretchen," I said sternly. "You are a very dirty girl. I suggest you get those clothes off and hop in. You reek of the barn. Come on, now. Do as I tell you—"

She stared at me, but her hands wouldn't let go of what she had dreamed of and wanted for so long. It's like that with dreamers.

"In the tub? The two of us—how is that possible?"

"Live and learn. Dealey says you can't make love in the water, but I've proven that old Limey expert wrong a thousand times. Come on. Last one in's a dairymaid." Even as I talked to her I was pulling the goods out of her peasant blouse. The idea was getting better and better. To hell with Mamma Marlene. She wouldn't have a sperm cell to stand on. Meantime I could rescue Gretchen from the pitfalls of virginity. My date with tall, blonde Christina Ketch was a long way off. So was the solution to silver pill enigmas. Which right then didn't mean a thing to me.

One thing about virgins. Maybe they wait a long time, but when that time comes, they really move. Gretchen got her clothes and underthings off like one of those lightning-fast comedy routines in a Keystone Cops comedy. She was standing beside a pile of lace, cotton and stockings and shoes. Naked, she was gorgeous. The chest line flared and flounced. Two beaming, lovely globules with each rosy areola seeming to smile. She was still bashful, though. Her hands had strayed down to her Venus mound in the classic September Morn pose. But all that did, like with the dame on the calendar, was to throw her creamy, marvelous ass further out. She was as curved as a scenic railway, for all the baby fat, but her body was spotlessly white and unblemished. Like a bottle of milk or a bar of fresh butter. I began to drool a little.

Maybe I'm the expert, but each time has something of the first time in it. After all, the girl was new. Anything could happen and just might. I could have one of the times of my life. And so could she!

"Come on in," I urged her. "The water's fine. Just tepid enough to be unnoticeable."

She stalled. "What will you do to me, Herr Damon?" She sounded like a squeaky little kid. That wouldn't do. So I laid the family jewels across the rim of the tub and held out my arms to her.

"Stop calling me *Herr*. I'm Rod. As you shall see. Now just follow the yellow brick road. Spelling optional . . . *Gretchennnnnn*. . . ."

That did it. The low, fervent husk of my pleading voice.

She dropped her hands, shuddered once and sprang forward, clearing the rim of the wooden tub and coming down with a splashing, flying flurry of all the good things she was endowed with. I met her with open arms. I had thought to indoctrinate her slowly and carefully so as not to hurt or alarm her. But little did I know. She was way ahead of me. She threw a hammer-lock around my neck, planted her red, panting lips on my mouth and submerged with me into the foot of bath water. And then her long, fleshy, hungry thighs wrapped around me in a pretzel-like vise and before I could say Howdy, she had impaled herself. With me. Right on target. A long, sliding, slithery, walloping line drive straight into the furry, glory gardens. She didn't scream or cry out, either. She just kept her mouth mashed onto mine and then began to piston like a dynamo. Her Teutonic take-charge attitude, which all Germans seem to be born with, brooked no denial. So she brooked and brooked and all I had to do was supply the artillery. I let her have her first round. She needed it. The water threshed, exploded and bubbled mightily. Gretchen's coming-out party, the going-in one, was tremendous and tidal. The wooden vat rocked and rolled. And all I did was stay stiff, swell and pound back.

Then her body shuddered, collapsed and she began to cry. It was the season for crying, it seemed. Maybe it was in the air. Or the beer.

Then she stopped crying, just as quickly, and relaxed. Like a dead man's float. She was face down in the water now and it was intoxicating to watch the liquid lap at her superbly arched buttocks, rivuleting and rilling in

46

and around her two mighty hillocks. The small of her back was no wider than one of my hands stretched out. I rubbed her back and she giggled in the water.

"Scuba-duba," I said. "Come up for air now. You don't want to get it waterlogged."

She rolled over like a porpoise at play and as narrow as the tub was she pulled my face down to her, mashing it against the lovely twin hills of her chest. It was like floating on your own life preservers. This kid could *never* drown. It just wasn't possible.

"Ah, *liebchen.* . . ." All the German endearments began to spill out of her. My women are always grateful. Especially the virgins. And this one hadn't seen nothin' yet! "Rod, *das ist so gut.* . . ."

"Ready to try the bed now?" I asked. "We don't need towels. I'll show you a great way to dry off . . . the *love* way."

She stopped moaning, blinked again and her breasts rose and fell with excitement. Nothing like me, obviously, had ever found its way to Munich and *The King's Inn.* Not since G.I. Joe went marching home.

"No towels? You make joke with me?"

"I never joke about sex."

"But, but—"

"Upsy-daisy. You first. Get on the bed and wait for me. Have I got a surprise for you!"

She was my slave. She did as I told her. She shot to the bed like Native Dancer, plopped down, spread-eagled herself and waited for me. I followed soon after. Approaching that eiderdown, pillow-stuffed fourposter was one of the delights of my Munich stay. To see Gretchen like that. Poised, ready, willing and able, her fine, big body still stipled with beads of moisture from the bath, her blonde hair in disarray, all her goodies in full view and waiting, was the pot of gold at the end of the rainbow.

And as I walked toward her, I grew and grew and grew.

Her eyes were amazed but she was speechless. I could see her pink tongue wetting her lips nervously. The water was fun, but this was the acid test. The water was

47

like a kid's game. But this was a bed. The place of trial.
The moment of truth.

I stalked her. Just like Ordonez with a brave bull in
Majorca. She quivered, shivering, not knowing what I
was going to do. She had kept her eyes closed in the tub.
She didn't dare close them now. I relished the moment,
reveled in the throbbing apparition of her chest. Her
long thighs were twitching nervously. Her navel danced.
The glory mound bristled, for all its dampness. Her tiny
waist was undulating. I could hear her catching her breath.
She was in thrall. I had her by the nuts.

So I got down at the end of the bed and began to
blow softly on her toes. I kept on blowing, fanning a
warm breath over her as I gradually moved up the line.
I waited and teased and waited and teased. And each
hot breath made her body jerk in frenzy—Nay, in ecstasy—so that she was out of her mind by the time my
questing mouth reached her knees, and then inched ever
so slowly up the high trail toward the bonanza. That did
it, and nowhere in Greek erotica is there anything to
compare with the *Kiss And Softly Blow* syndrome. Believe me, it changed Roman history.

"Ahhhhhhhhhh—!" Gretchen cried out, gasping.

Just as I met the man in the boat, that delicate little
muscle which lies waiting in the female clitoris, and my
tongue rolled it with loving care and attention, Gretchen
went ape.

Her thighs spread out in a V that I thought would
surely break them; she tried to rise up to grab my face
and pull it down, but I was way ahead of her. After
all, I'd been there before. She hadn't. I was the pro.

She was as open as she would ever be and there was
no more time to kid around. I swept her ankles up in
both hands, passing her thighs above my shoulders. I
raised my hips on high for *The Damon Drop* and I went
up, up as far as the law of gravity allowed. Gretchen's
eyeballs did a loop-the-loop of fear and uncomprehen-
sion. And that was the moment.

I dive-bombed from the ceiling at the almost perpen-
dicular angle that amazes sexologists the world over and
entered her. But what an entry! Guns should go off,
trumpets blare, fanfares roll, when you hit them with

that one. You go in up to your elbows. Pushing, thrusting, rocketing, bursting and all the glory hole can do is widen, widen, widen to accept the gift. It must surround you with marshy gratitude or perish.

There was a fast, furious fusion of both of our bodies and poor Gretchen was overwhelmed. She lanced back at me, arching almost to break her back and her great breasts and buttocks tried to withstand the assault. But they couldn't. *The Damon Drop* once put Madame de la Roni away in Naples and that old pro had had her ashes hauled a million times when I got to her. So it goes. They're all only human, after all is laid and done.

Gretchen did, once again, the only thing possible, considering her green salad history.

She let out one hoarse bleat of mad ecstasy.

And fainted again.

It figured.

Too much of a good thing at the very onset of knowledge and pleasure would knock anybody out. Gretchen Zimmer was no exception. And she'd done plenty all right for herself, for a first time around the block.

I felt marvelous. Other guys keep fit by making with the barbells, lifting weights or doing push-ups. Well, I like my own weapons. Nothing beats going the route with two or three women every day. That's the way to stay in shape; anyhow, it is the Damon Physical Fitness Prescription. Try it some time. You'll never have to watch the waistline or the calories, believe me. I'm programmed for sex.

Gretchen didn't wake up for a full hour, so I busied myself for the coming evening. Going over Walrus-moustache's report, laying out my clothes, selecting a sportscoat, slacks and turtleneck shirt for the bar routine where I had to contact Christina Ketch. I never carry a gun of any kind. I believe in my own built-in weapon. Guns are okay but I don't go in for killing. Like I told you, I'm a lover not a low serial number.

It got to be about five o'clock and Gretchen stirred on the big bed. Mamma hadn't come looking for her. Like I expected. *The King's Inn* was like a peaceful, sleepy hamlet. Nothing but cocks crowing in the barn, cows mooing and chickens clucking. From the window,

I couldn't see any vehicles of any kind coming up the country road. All was quiet on the Munich front. The gray day was dying, fading into a dark, dark Bavarian night.

Gretchen didn't say a word. She got up from the bed, staggered to the pile of clothes and began to dress slowly. Her movements were confused and dazed. Like a woman moving in a dream.

"Okay, my *strudel?*" I asked. She nodded. When she finally got reasonably presentable for the outside world, she lurched into my arms and hugged me. Her body shuddered and her massive breasts rippled against me. For a second I thought she was going to raise her skirts.

"You going to cry again?"

"*Nein!* For why? You make me so happy!"

"Good. What time do things get jumping downstairs?"

"Seven o'clock. Everybody comes. The burgers. The teamsters. The villagers. Tourists too. I shall make you a glass of our wine. You will see. It goes to your head."

I held her off at arm's length and looked at her. She blushed and lowered her eyes. Her full cheeks were flaming red.

"You're much woman, Gretchen. But don't tell Mamma. Understand?"

She wagged her head in a furious negative. "Damn right! I tell her, she want you for herself. Mamma is crazy for a good man—oh, Rod! Tell me. Was I really *good?*"

"In a word, yes."

"And you will let me be good again? Before you go? You will show me some more of the three hundred ways in your book?"

"If there is time—fifty at least."

She nearly swooned but I held her tight, kissed her again, patted her on the rump; and sighing, but happy as a lark with fifteen worms, she tripped gayly out of the room. This time she shot the bolt open with a defiant slam of sound. Then she winked, laughed out loud and was gone. But not forgotten.

But she would keep until I needed her late that night.

Meanwhile, I made myself ready for Christina Ketch, Girl Spy. I wondered what the hell *she* would be like.

CHAPTER FIVE

The King's Inn was really jumping when I sashayed downstairs after seven o'clock to get the lay of the land. The place was a sort of old-fashioned meeting place, after all. The eating and drinking that was going on was protean. Never have I seen so many village types, complete with pipes and tankards, having a helluva good time. Somebody was pumping away on an accordion, and several lusty, red-faced rubes were raising their voices in song. It wasn't the *Horst Wessel Song* or *Deutschland Uber Alles* but even if it had been, I wouldn't have been too surprised. Nazism isn't that dead in the Rhineland.

Nobody paid too much attention to me, so I parked myself in a corner booth, complete with lamplight and curtains and wooden table covered with a speakeasy-style cloth. As I figured, Gretchen Zimmer, all dolled up in ribbons and a cute peasant dress that barely concealed her whim-whams, was doubling in brass. Rushing back and forth, filling all orders for food and another peek-a-boo at her low-cut blouse. Mamma Marlene was doing what came naturally. Circulating among the paying customers, joking, laughing, adding her gusty voice to all the good humor and fun. Sort of a German Texas Guinan. I didn't expect less from her. If she didn't know how to turn a fast buck I would have been surprised. There was just too damn much *Cabaret* in her make-up. I would have bet she saw Dietrich in *The Blue Angel* a dozen times.

The singing patrons had worked their way into *Lili Marlene,* that old World War Two goodie, when Gretchen came tripping over to my table. I was keeping an eye peeled for Christian Ketch. So far there was no one in the place that answered her description. Most of the dames already present were fat, over-blown and ruddy-pussed. My lady fair of skin had not shown up yet.

"A glass of wine, my darling?" Gretchen whispered, bending over me so I could get a fine look at the hills of home.

"Why not? Pour me your best."

She winked. "For you—the best. You deserve it."

"I agree. I'm thirsty. Hop to it."

She sauntered off and Mamma Marlene, from a table nearby, flung me a knowing look. Her big smile was all teeth. Mamma figured the net was dropping fast. I waved back, the perfect fool. And while I was waving, a tall, very large, very beautiful specimen of femininity suddenly was in the crowded room, threading her way between the tables, looking for a quiet corner. My senses jangled to attention. This had to be the contact. The hair was flaxen-gold and long; the skin incredibly white. I couldn't see all of the figure, for a loose, sloppy trenchcoat covered the merchandise. A soft, battered Tyrolean cap rode jauntily on the golden head.

As luck would have it, she had to pass my table.

I waited for her to come. Nobody was paying much attention to her, either. In places like Munich, great-looking blondes are a dime a dozen.

She had drawn abreast of my table, her fine blue eyes still trying to find an empty table. I looked up at her and for a moment, our eyes locked. She had regular features. Straight nose, strong chin and a tilt to her sullen red mouth. She hesitated, knowing I was going to say something. Or make a pass, at the very least.

I quoted Walrus-moustache's code line verbatim:

"What's a nice girl like you doing in a Bavarian joint like this?"

She didn't bat an eye.

"Waiting for lightning to hit my rod," she murmured.

I stood up and she sat down. She did it quickly, without fuss. She squared her shoulders, pyramided her hands and waited for me to sit down again. I did. At best, anyone would have thought she was a nearsighted beauty who hadn't recognized her date until she had practically stumbled over him.

"Hi, Chris," I said, trying to make friends right away.

She scowled. "You will call me Miss Ketch, if you please."

"Is that really necessary? After all, being fellow-agents and all——"

"Hush, you fool!" She hissed at me. "So. The great

52

Damon hasn't learned how to behave even at this late date. Don't you realize what they do to spies? Be sensible, man, and mind your manners. This is not a lark."

"I groaned. A G.I. chicken-shit female was what Walrus-moustache had handed me for an ally. *That* I didn't need. I mumbled something and stared at my hands.

I tried to make the peace, though. I owed it to Walrus-moustache and the Thaddeus X. Coxe Foundation.

"Have a wine," I said. "They say this place is famous for——"

"Order me a glass of milk," she said flatly.

"Okay. And some wieners and sauerkraut?"

"Ugh. Disgusting food. Order me a sandwich. Two slices of bread, one thin sliver of cheese."

I controlled myself. Gretchen was coming back. Smiling, bearing a metal tray with my tall glass of red wine reflecting the lamps of the inn. When she saw I wasn't alone, she almost crowned me with the tray. I hastened to make amends. Christina Ketch barely glanced up at her. She was tightening the stem on her wristwatch—I think.

I ordered the milk and sandwich, winked at Gretchen to show her I was just being sociable and that assuaged her a little. But she gave me a furious. warning look. Jealousy. All I needed. My new-found cold fish acquaintance didn't have a jot of female warmth to spare.

"Did you hear the one about the guy working in a pickle factory who was stuck with the boss' wife in the basement and when he finds out she doesn't like pickles, he has to——"

My attempt to warm things up with a lively joke got me a response I couldn't have expected. The creamy beauty of Christina Ketch's lovely face flushed a beet red. Her lips compressed and her nostrils pinched. The look she shot across the table at me was sheer venom. As Gretchen walked away to fill the order, she hissed, "Do not tell me any jokes. Not ever. I find them disgusting and asinine. Understood?"

I showed her my teeth. "You want me to salute and say, Yes, sir!?"

"I want you to stop being silly and be an adult."

"All right." I gave up. "Now, here's my plan——"

"No, here is my plan, she said evenly in clipped tones. "I have our orders. I also have a Renault parked outside. It will get us to the border, then to Betchnika. We will travel as man and wife. Tourists, ostensibly. I speak French, German and Czech. We shall be able to scour the town and make inquiries. All you have to do is accompany me and keep your mouth shut. I know you speak only English. I don't know why they saddled me with a man like you, but I intend to make the best of it. You understand?"

The hairs on the back of my neck rose. My feathers were ruffled, but good. Who the hell did this bitch think she was? A commissar?

"Now, look here, you fugitive from a Greta Garbo movie," I snarled. "I'll have you know that I'm considered a top——"

"Shut up," she. commanded tersely. "Here comes that simple-faced waitress again. By the way, I will drive the car, I will make all the arrangements. Understood? You are second in command. I will work no other way. If this mystery about the silver pill is to be solved and we need to learn why those men were lynched, it will be necessary that I lead the investigation."

I was spluttering when Gretchen slammed the plates and glass down. She was mad too. She stalked off without saying anything or waiting for us to ask her anything. Christina Ketch calmly attacked her cheese on pumpernickel, sipped her milk with detachment, as unconcerned as the bird on the wing. I downed my Bavarian wine at a gulp, to stop the sputters and to keep from choking. Miss Christina Ketch simply went down the wrong way. She *bugged* me.

"Any questions?" Christina Ketch asked tersely.

I stared at her. It was unbelievable.

"Why, you—you—" I couldn't get to the right word to describe her.

"Control yourself. I'll bring you through this alive. But only if you obey me."

That did it. Not even the Coxe Foundation or threat of exposure as a carnal sexologist could make me put up with this kind of treatment at the hands of a mere, ordinary dame.

54

"Listen, you steel-plated secret agent," I snarled again. "I'm not going anywhere with you. I quit. Go get yourself another boy. Where I come from, dames know their place. Who the hell do you think you are? Better still, I'm firing you. You, I don't need. I'll take the waitress with me on this assignment, as dumb as she is. I didn't come all the way to Germany to be bossed around by a modernday Ilse Koch. Screw you, sister. I'm getting out—"

Christina Ketch sighed.

"You are ridiculous. You can't 'fire' me, as you call it. We are both under instructions. Top priority. You want to get shot?"

"Better dead than led. Get me? Pack up, baby, and beat it."

She almost smiled.

"All right. I have disturbed your male ego. Very well. I recognize that bourgeois instinct. I will not yield to it. But I shall challenge it. Are you game, Mr. Damon, for a test? Brute force against brute force? We shall see who is the stronger of us two?"

"Are you for real, lady? What the hell are you talking about?"

Christina Ketch froze me with a look.

"You are a man, I suppose. You imagine yourself stronger than me. Very well, then. I say you are not, and to prove my claim, I challenge you to a test of strength." She reached out and moved the breadsticks and plates away, leaving a clearing in the center of the table. "Give me your hand." She was dead serious.

I stared at her, mouth open. She was resting her elbow on the table, arm up, right hand extended. Unless I was nuts or already drunk on Gretchen Zimmer's Bavarian wine special, she wanted to hand wrestle me, Indian style!

I restrained a smirk and set my elbow next to hers. I grabbed her hand almost jubilantly. Right then and there it would have given me the greatest pleasure to break her arm. Her fingers were cool and pliable.

"You're sure now?" I teased. "You know what you're giving up? You lose and I'm the boss of this enterprise. It's only fair to warn you in advance, I was a four-letter man in college."

55

"Yes," she sneered. "And I know what those letters are. F-U-C-K. You fool. Save your strength. You're going to need it!"

"Says who?"

"Ready?" She ignored my sally, her eyes boring into mine. "Go!"

Never in my life have I been so embarrassed. Not even when I was caught in the bedroom of the dean's wife at that same college I was bragging about, helping her put in a light bulb. The fact that we were naked at the time did little to convince anyone of my innocence. But that red face was nothing compared to what happened now in *The King's Inn*.

Not only did I lose the Indian hand wrestling contest to Christina Ketch, I never even worked up a small bead of sweat on her marble brow!

And it all happened so fast.

One second I had her hand vised in mine, laughing on the inside, and the next, she merely flexed whatever secret weapon she had and I was straining like an old woman to keep from having my hand slammed down on the checkerboard table cloth. She had rippling steel in her fingertips. I could feel the muscles popping in my right arm. And then it was all over. Without a smile, her arm twitched and Bingo!—my hand shot down. Flat and out. I let out a howl. I had to. I felt something give in my wrist. As well as my Ego.

"What's the matter?" she asked acidly. "Did I hurt you?"

"Geezis, you're mean," I blurted. "You damn near broke my wrist!"

She almost had, too. I had a king-sized strain. No matter how much I wagged and wiggled my fingers and arm, my wrist ached. Which was just peachy. On top of losing to her, she had managed to cripple me, even if only temporarily.

"There," she said. "Then it's all settled. I give the orders. Are we agreed?"

"A bet's a bet," I said sullenly, the good loser. "I'll keep my part of the bargain, but if I ever found out you cheated, watch out, sister! I'll pound your poop into oblivion."

She wasn't buffaloed, returning to the remains of her cheese on pumpernickel and the glass of milk.

"There was no need to resort to wiles. I have nothing up my sleeve except my arm, I can assure you. I am strong. Stronger than you. Now I will lead. And my first set of instructions are these: as soon as we have finished dining, we will go out to the Renault and drive to the Czechoslovakian border."

"You said it, you tomboy, you."

We finished the meal in silence. I had no more to say to her. My wrist hurt, my ego was dented out of shape, and not even Gretchen's dirty looks as she waited on the other tables, bothered me. *Frau* Marlene Zimmer was whooping it up with some of the villagers, laughing, singing, and whipping her skirts up, like any floozy. The singing of songs and playing of music went on, *ad nauseum*. I wanted Out in a hurry. The sooner we scrammed, the better. The wine in my system hadn't had a chance to catch hold. I was too mad to feel good.

Finally Christina Ketch was touching her red lips with a napkin, brushing crumbs from her fingers, and standing up. I got up too. I felt a little bit better about losing then, but not much. The broad was a good five feet ten inches and as big as a big girl can be. I wondered exactly what the trenchcoat was hiding. I had a rough idea though. She was probably built like the Berlin Wall. She had to be. Nobody had ever beat me at Indian hand wrestling. Not ever.

Surprisingly, nobody paid any attention to our leaving. That is, not until we were almost up to the Dutch door entrance. And then all hell broke loose. I thought we were slipping out as easy as pie but I did not reckon on Mamma Zimmer and her darling little Gretchen. Christina Ketch and I were just stepping through the entrance when a flurry of skirts and outraged cries made us turn around. And there was Mamma Marlene, in all her drunken glory, a little the worse for Bavarian wine intake, arms folded, face flushed and belligerently righteous. Behind her, a tearful Gretchen stared pleadingly at me over Mamma's shoulder. But the rest of *The King's Inn* was too drunk and far gone to take any interest in the show going on up front. *"Liebchen,"* Gretchen whimpered, a lost soul.

"So," Mamma Marlene said in an ugly voice. "Bummer! Low-lifer! You kitchy-koo my Gretchen and then run off with another hussy. No, you don't! You must stay and do the right thing!"

"I already have," I began lamely. "But you see I just inherited a million dollars because my old uncle died and this nice lady is taking me to the lawyer's office and——"

"You promised!" Gretchen suddenly wailed. "You said you would show me the three hundred ways to make love—" Woefully, she reddened.

"Aha!" Mamma Zimmer whooped. "You see? Stay and be a man, *Herr* Damon!" In her excitement, she clutched her own breasts.

Christina Ketch said quietly, "We are leaving. Do not try to stop us. Come, Damon. The car is just outside."

But hell hath no fury like an outraged Mamma trying to unload a daughter. Mamma Zimmer raced around us, dragging Gretchen with her and she blocked the Dutch door. Her eyes rolled to heaven, asking Judgment.

"You are not going," she panted. "Not until this man saves my daughter's good name—"

"Get out of the way," Christina Ketch said coldly. "I'm warning you for the last time."

"Girls, girls," I begged. "Please—" It was all too much for Gretchen. She started to cry. At the top of her big voice. That wouldn't do. Christina Ketch liked it even less than I did. I tried to step in, but my new leader was way ahead of me. Way way ahead.

I never saw either of the punches. One had to be a right hook and the other a left cross, considering where Mamma Zimmer and her Gretchen were standing in the doorway. But all I could see was a blur and jet movement of the Ketch shoulders. And then, both Zimmer dollies were flat on their keisters in the doorway and Christina Ketch had grabbed my other wrist and was dragging me out to safety and freedom.

"Come on," she snapped. "We'll have to run now before those loyal customers come to the rescue. March!"

I didn't need any urging.

Feeling like a criminal, a rat and three kinds of a stinker, I allowed Christina Ketch to bum's rush me out of the inn. The darkness was new and inky-black. There was no moon and only the lights of the tavern guiding us. I spotted the Renault parked under a tree, next to a hay cart and a motorcycle. Behind us, there was a sudden uproar and tumult of confusion. The terrible deed had been discovered. Someone had put the slug on Mamma and her daughter—I could see and hear it all. But my leader was quick and efficient. In no time at all, she had leaped into the Renault, made room for me, had the machine in gear and racing in less time than it takes to open a pack of *Sheiks*.

I never did see the wild scene at the inn because the Renault was off to the races long before anyone could come out and shout at us or throw a bottle of Bavarian wine. There was no pursuit, of course. Those rummies couldn't have found a tree in Central Park, the condition they had to be in. So I left *The King's Inn* without regret. After all, dear Gretchen hadn't done too badly for herself at that. She'd had the screw of a lifetime and now maybe the swains of her village would come to know what she really had to offer. Why waste it?

Mamma Marlene would survive somehow. The old dolls always do. And at thirty-nine, she had the world of sex by the balls. It's got to be the best year of a woman's life.

The night was cool and breezy. Darkened roads swept by, the shadowy peaks of the mountainous range loomed on the horizon. Christina Ketch drove with rare skill. She seemed to know every bump and sinkhole in the roadway. We didn't hit a single one.

So there we were. Speeding in the dead of night for the Czech border. Toward who the hell knew what. And I was second-in-command of a two-person spy detail. What a life. All I had for a boss was a human robot of incredible strength, who could beat me at anything physical, I suspected, thought nothing of decking two harmless women, and drove a car like Stirling Moss. What a gorgeous deal I had got myself flummoxed into. At least on previous assignments for the Coxemen, I had been my own boss. Now I was less than that.

With a sprained wrist, besides.

Suddenly Christina Ketch spoke up, without taking her eyes off the road.

59

"Did you really have intercourse with that dairymaid?"

"Yes, I did. Want to make something of it?"

She laughed harshly. "What a cow. How could you?"

"It's very easy. Want me to show you how it's done?" I inquired with sheer acid and venom. "First you take off that trenchcoat—"

"You will never have me, Damon. I don't need you. I am dedicated to the cause. All I want for us to have is a sensible, working relationship to uncover the enigma of these silver pills. Understood?"

"Ah," I said, disgustedly, closing my eyes and slumping in my narrow seat. "Blow it out of your barracks bag, will you, lady? Just wake me up when we get to the Czech border."

So that's how Christina Ketch and I hit it off the first time we were alone. With sarcasm, scorn and mutual hatred and disrespect.

Ain't that a dandy way to go into battle to meet the enemy?

But I had a secret, anyway.

I was two up on my emotionless blonde colleague, whether she knew it or not. During my crowded career I have managed to pick up a few things besides all there is to know about the subject of Sex. I didn't know where she got her information about me, but English is not my only language.

I speak French too.

And Russian.

Which meant I could curse her in all three languages.

And, boys and girls, I was saving up some pretty good ones.

All the way on the midnight ride toward the sleeping Czech border where you still need passports and luck to get in. Those damn Reds run a country pretty tight once they become landlords.

But my time would come with Christina Ketch. That I promised myself even as I tried to take a nap in the little car racing toward the mountains.

Visions of her trying to run away from me bare-assed with me in hot pursuit, ran around in my head. I know my women. I know sex. If the trenchcoat was hiding a decent figure to match the lovely face, I could sweeten her

60

disposition up in no time at all with a little of my special whoopee brand of love-making. I've brought out the best in hundreds of broads. All I had to do was get her to where she *had* to look at the family jewels. If that didn't make her mouth water, then she was a hopeless case altogether.

You bet your bippy!

CHAPTER SIX

It took us two and a half hours to get to Betchnika. That is, it took Christina Ketch that long. As fine a car as the Renault was, and as skilled a driver as Boss Lady might be, the roads to that town were winding, narrow and loaded with jughandle curves as the highway climbed up toward the mountains and beyond. She didn't whimper or complain, either. Or talk a helluva lot to me except to bark out orders like, *"Roll up your window; it's cold"* or *"Open the window; it's muggy in here"* or *"do not smoke; I detest tobacco!"* and last but not least, *"If you try to touch my knee again, I'll break your arm, Damon."* See? A real ace doll, all the way. A sweetheart. Kind, calm and delicious. Oh, yeah.

I'd had to give up trying to sleep. The Renault bounced on the rutted roads like a steer hopped up with loco weed. And the night was dark and unfriendly and considerably colder, the higher above sea level we got. Oh, it was a peachy journey.

When we hit the border and stopped in front of one of those striped roadway fences that goes up and down like an elevator with sentry box to match, Christina Ketch also did all the talking. I was past caring. The booted, uniformed, armed guards who sidled over with ugly faces to look at our papers weren't the sort of heartwarming guys I like to chat with. So I sat and said nothing, trying to look stupid. But I listened in amazement as she rattled off what sounded like pure Czech dialogue, flashed an impressively thick set of leather visas and even made some small talk with the guards. They liked her, for some weird reason, and were laughing when they waved her on through. I had my suspicions. Not of the visas. Walrus-moustache and the Coxe Foundation prepare all assignments like field generals, but I did wonder what the guards had found to laugh about.

"What did you tell them?" I gritted as she ploughed on toward Betchnika, giving the Renault the gas. "That I'm your looney hubby and you're taking me to Betchnika for the cure?"

She shook her head, almost smiling.

"No. But a good guess. I told them you had a cyst on your rump and were going to see Dr. Mandel in Betchnika to have it lanced."

"I got one all right and you're it." I snorted. "Is there a Dr. Mandel?"

"Of course not. What would they know? They are only guards on a border post. Interested only in defectors trying to leave, contraband, and fugitives from justice."

"I see. By the way, not that it is important, but since you have the visas and are running this show, who exactly are we supposed to be?"

Her eyes flew to the speedometer then back to the road. She was one business-like broad. It was almost midnight now, but lights were beginning to show like fireflies through the wall of trees. The town where the silver pill mystery had come to pass couldn't be very far away. I was glad. I was tired, hungry and bored. And I was going to call Walrus-moustache on the hot line, first chance I got. Though I didn't expect that to be until tomorrow morning.

"Well, answer my question," I growled. "Who are we?"

"Mr. and Mrs. Walter Gotkin. I am Emily Gotkin. We are German citizens. West German, naturally. You are a clerk in the Diesmann Travel Agency. We have come to Betchnika to see about that cyst and to visit your dying mother."

"Swell. Do we see this mother?"

"No. It is only a cover story. No one bothers much about Betchnika. It is a small town in the middle of nowhere. Rather like your little towns out West in America. Now keep quiet. I have just enough petrol to get us to town and I have to gauge it or you shall be getting out and pushing us all the way in."

"Mrs. Gotkin, I have news for you."

"Yes? What is it?"

"I want a divorce."

There was no more to say. We were unfriendly enemies stuck in the same job. But none of my remarks ever got her goat. I could see that too. She had the upper hand in everything. She was in command; she knew the language; she obviously knew the town. What the hell could I do? I had to let her call the shots, whether I liked it or not—at least until I got in touch with Walrus-moustache.

Betchnika looked like a ghost village when we got in. There were hardly any lights, the roadway was far from improved or modern, and the tallest building was about four stories high. The street-corner lamps were dim and spooky. We seemed to be the only ones abroad. I guessed it was one of those towns where they roll the sidewalks up at nine o'clock and everybody goes to bed. It was hard to tell. Some fog had rolled down from the mountains and it was a pea-soup entrance. But somewhere, somehow, Christina Ketch knew exactly where she was going. She slowed the Renault down, eased into a driveway of sorts that was flanked by two rows of low trees, and braked to a halt. I was stiff all over and my sprained wrist hadn't gotten much better. Nor had my masculine pride.

"Now what?" I asked.

"The Hotel Betchnika," she said, curtly, climbing out her side of the car. "This is where we will stay to conduct our investigation. Come. I have a suitcase in the trunk. You will carry it in."

It was then and only then did I realize that we had fled *The King's Inn,* leaving my Jad bag and attaché case behind. The case with the thick report on the silver pill. Jeezis, that was clever. I almost groaned aloud. I felt like three kinds of a jackass.

"What is wrong now, Damon?"

"You hijacked me out of that tavern, and all that accomplished was to leave my luggage and everything important behind, get it? Swell, right? What do I do for clothes?"

"That's no concern of mine. In expediency, one has to act fast. You have funds. Tomorrow you can shop in

63

town. It will provide a good excuse for asking questions."

"If you say so," I shivered in my turtleneck shirt and light sportscoat. "Lead on, Macduff."

"Remember to sign the register as Mr. and Mrs. Walter Gotkin. We must be careful now. This is enemy territory."

"Don't I know it?"

She would have been funny except for being so heartless. Chilled to the bone, I followed her into the Hotel Betchnika. I wasn't expecting the Grand Hotel so I didn't get it.

There was one potted plant, a wall poster that advertised some kind of flower festival for the next week, and a battered carpet and a wooden desk with lots of empty pigeonholes behind the counter. Also, one sleepy-faced old man trying to doze by the switchboard. The elevator, a real fly cage, was just hidden behind the potted plant. It was a hotel, all right, like from way back when, and smaller than a breadbox.

The old-timer wasn't surprised to see us, or glad, or dismayed, or anything. Shuddering out of fatigue, he turned the register around for me to sign, indicated pen and ink, and kept on yawning. Then he handed me a key and went back to sleep. The register was an eye-opener. There were three people registered, all singles. Probably the town drunk, the sheriff and the bellboy.

But there wasn't a bellboy.

I carried Christina Ketch's luggage, which was no more than a wicker suitcase, as light as feathers, and we took the elevator up. To the top floor, which was the fourth one. We had Room 7. But it didn't sound lucky to me, even though I had begun to wonder what the sleeping arrangements might be. After all, Ketch and I, to keep up the front, would have to share a room together all night. Maybe, one bed. Betchnika didn't look like the sort of town that could afford double beds. It also didn't seem like the sort of burg where twenty-five old-timers had been lynched, either. Or the road to silver pills.

Surprisingly, Number 7 was a large room that faced the street and lights, and was reasonably clean and airy. The wallpaper was atrocious and peeling a little, and a crock of pitcher water sat on the oaken bureau dresser where it reflected itself in a spidery-glassed mirror. Christina Ketch grunted something under her breath, locked the door and marched around to the other side of the bed. She didn't say a word but began to undress quickly. Like a very business-like call girl in a cheap hotel.

I stared, dumbfounded—nay, fascinated.

She was behaving as if she were alone. I watched the trenchcoat fall away and blinked. She'd looked big in *The King's Inn* but not even I was prepared for the Amazon standing revealed before me in a Sloppy Joe sweater, coarse wool skirt and knee-length stockings. She ruffled her golden-blonde bobbed hair and when she stretched her arms, her chest was fantastic. A forty-four, at least. This led down into hips that simply flared and flared and flared. I coughed.

She stopped taking off her stockings and stared at me, questioningly, again a call girl, wondering why her customer was surprised.

"Yes?" Like I said, her face was lovely, but it was too perfect to be real. The skin was supremely right, the mouth as red as tomatoes, the eyes as blue as the Mediterranean.

"About the bed," I said. "I do not intend to sleep on the floor."

"You don't have to. We will share the bed. But I warn you. That is all we will share. I like the right so you shall have the left. But keep to your side. One gesture, one false move—and I will break your arm, I promise you." I could see she meant it too. She was glaring.

"Don't you believe in sex?"

"Yes, I do. But not with a fellow agent when there is work to be done. I do not wish to become interested in you as a man. Understand? It would cloud my mind, affect my reason. I warn you, Damon. Do not make the mistake of not taking me seriously. Or that sometime tonight you will arouse me in the dark as I sleep, with your fingers, or your lips, or your penis. If you do, you will regret it. It has all been tried on me before and I have been known to castrate a man. So be on your guard. Now, hurry and get to bed and turn out the lights. We have much to do tomorrow and we will need some sleep. It is already past midnight."

With that, she turned her back on me and disrobed quickly. The sweater, the skirt and everything else. But she wore no bra or panties and before I went into the little bathroom off the bedroom to get a glass of water, I saw an ass that was out of this world. Out of this universe.

She had her own set of Bavarian Alps. And they weren't snow-covered or cold-looking. I bit my lower lip in frustration. I have never gone to bed without getting my ashes hauled. But tonight looked like the night! I believed everything she had told me. She was as hard as nails and all I had to remember was the merciless, matter-of-fact way she had floored the Zimmer ladies. *Pow! Pow!*

So I undressed. Down to the buff.

I marched out to the bedroom, walked around to her side of the bed, where the light was, to turn them off. It was my last feeble attempt. I was riding high as I always was, standing out front and center and she couldn't have missed the phenomenon. She was facing me, hugging her pillow, watching me as I reached for the light switch. Her naked shoulder gleamed up at me. But if I expected admiration and hunger in her eyes, I was sorely disappointed. Scorn shone there and her perfect mouth curled in a sneer of disgust. She was sleeping in the raw too, but a helluva lot of good that was going to do me.

"Ugh," she said. "You're a freak. What a sickening thing to carry about one's person all day long!"

"What's wrong with it?" I blurted. "It's all me!"

"I can see that and I feel sorry for you. Go sit in a cold tub of water or whatever you have to do. Masturbate or drop the window on that abomination. You ought to be ashamed of yourself. You call yourself an agent? Go to Denmark and have an operation. It would be better for everyone. But before you do all that, please turn out the lights. I am very tired."

"Why, you, you—" I spluttered.

She closed her eyes, bored with me, indifferent to my charm or my soul. Or my desires.

"Just remember what I said. My body is tempting and pleasing, I know. But if you so much as touch me while we sleep, you will be a sorry, sorry man. I sprained your wrist, remember? Well, I can also break that rude thing off and make you eat it. Good night, Mr. Damon."

She was through talking to me. She began to breathe deeply and the coverlet, just barely cresting her wondrous mammaries, began to rise and fall gently. For one terrible moment, rape found its way into my heart. I wanted to jump on her, spread her legs and pummel away for Old Glory, but I didn't have a flag and, I must admit, I was afraid of her. What with my sprained wrist and all, she probably would be able to do exactly what she threatened. The mere idea made me break out into a cold sweat. What a bitch!

Christina Ketch. Well, she was going to *ketch* it áll right. And I swore on a stack of my sexual manuals that I was going to be the guy who did the throwing. But not now. For a time, she had won. She was in control, but my day would come.

Her lay would come.

Meekly, I slid into the bed next to her. Fortunately it was a big bed for such a small hotel. I kept a good three feet away from her, but it was maddening to know that mere inches separated me from the biggest, creamiest derrière I had seen in years. Not even Gretchen Zimmer, for all her dairymaid largess, had had a behind to match the Ketch fanny. What a crying shame!

I could smell her too.

A warm healthy, dizzying animal aroma that exuded from her body. I was rigid with desire. My male ego, as she had said, was challenged. And since sex is mainly a mental stimuli before the actual action begins, I was in a helluva bad way. I was big enough to scale Mount Everest, hard enough to ram a steel bank vault, thick enough to wade my way through a wall of human flesh, dragging my testicles behind me.

I gritted my teeth and tried not to cry. My jaws grated.

"Damon," she said in the darkness, and my heart soared as cold and flat as her voice was. You can never be sure with dames.

"Yes?"

"I suppose you will lie there like a little boy all night and whine and whimper, so if you will allow me I shall

67

relieve your suffering. All right?" She sounded almost amused but I didn't care.

"Christina!"

"It's nothing, and I see it is necessary, so don't move and I will fix you up, as they say in your part of the world. Are we agreed?"

"Baby," I chortled, sure of my charm and convinced that all I had to do was get her started, make her see I was the man with the power, and she'd be eating out of my hand all the rest of the way in. Oh, yeah. Little did I know.

But I was lying back; I pulled the covers down and the horse sprang to the post, high enough to hang a hat on. Christina Ketch moved like an animal from her side of the bed and both her strong hands reached out and fastened themselves around the family jewels. Thrills shot through me. Red-hot, hungry expectation. And then she woke me up with a savage, wrenching, twisting application of that brute strength she had shone me in the tavern. You would have thought she was winding a watch!

Believe me, I can't explain the difference. You can lead a horse to water but you can't make him drink, the sages say. The canny sexologist will tell you: *nothing will kill an erection faster than the slightest pain.*

That's how she did it.

In five fast seconds, with brutal pivots and turns of her strong hands, she wrung me and bruised me until I was spattering impotently into the air, away from the bed, and finally she let go and I was moaning like a banshee. I felt like pulverized grapes and smashed bananas.

"There," she said flatly, triumphantly. "Now go wipe that mess off yourself, stop whining, and go to sleep. I warn you once again. I must get my rest or our stay here in Betchnika will be a complete waste of time. Understood?"

"Yeah," I rasped, fighting back the tears of pain. "Sleep tight, you bitch. I wouldn't touch you with a ten-foot pole."

"Good." She turned over on her side, away from me. "It's settled then. *Good night.*"

She was breathing deeply in no time at all. Untroubled,

undisturbed. Sure of herself. An iron butterfly. A brass cupcake. A steel-plated ice-cold Katie.

I lay there in the dark bruised, sore, madder than a wet rooster, and thinking up ways of killing her without leaving a trace. She hadn't only sprained my wrist; she had damned near put my dick in a sling. It was throbbing like a banjo, humming with an agony I had never experienced, not even the time I ran into a door in a dark bedroom because I thought my naked target was standing there. That had been years ago when I was a kid, but I had never forgotten it. No man ever would. A dong has a memory like an elephant's.

And dongs were made to be loved and handled with tender loving care.

Oh, how it hurt.

But all I could do was wait until the pain subsided and my anger calmed down. I would have to wait a little while longer, that was all. Oh, revenge would be sweet! There are many ways to skin a cat or trap a dame. I would just have to think of all them.

But first I would have to bury the notion of killing Christina Ketch. That would have to come later. First I would screw her until her ears flew off. And her eyeballs popped. That's the only proper answer for a snot-nosed, big-assed broad.

I must have fallen asleep while my vendetta formed in my mind. Hell, I couldn't stay up all night crying over spilled milk. Or misused semen. There was still tomorrow.

And I would never forgive Walrus-moustache for hitching my wagon to a cold star like Christina Ketch.

Never, never, never.

He should have known better!

Known *me* better.

In a world that practices oneupmanship, gamesmanship, and everybody is trying to put it up everybody else, there is one rule I follow with women. None of them ever get the best of me. I get to all of them—in the end.

And Christina Ketch was going to have the sorest rear end in town when I was through with her. Damon leads the pack in that individual skill known as sexmanship. Hell, I invented it.

. Mrs. Emily Gotkin was going to find out that the man

69

she had "married" had a lot of tricks in his bag. Not the least of which was the old ploy of an-eye-for-an-eye.

Silver pills, hell.

Betchnika, balls.

Damon, yes!

When my wrist got better and my shipping department restored to normal status, I had a few surprises for Miss Christina Ketch. Boy, was she in for it!

The only trouble with my kind of revenge is that it usually benefits the recipient of same. That's the curse of it. When Ketch got her comeuppance, all that would happen was that she would wind up enjoying herself as she couldn't possibly have had in her cold-fish lifetime.

But at least it would make a woman out of her.

I was willing to make the sacrifice for mankind.

There's a lot of humanitarianism in sex, no matter what the prudes, bluenoses and dire prophets say. I mean —where the hell would we all be if Eve hadn't dropped her fig leaf?

You see how it is.

A little piece of apple can go a long way.

Ask Adam.

He had 'em too!

CHAPTER SEVEN

Three horrible days and nights went by.

Betchnika became my Waterloo, Little Big Horn, and Dunkirk, all in one. And it was all Christina Ketch's fault. Not that she rubbed her supremacy in—she didn't have to. But the morning sunlight that beamed down on Betchnika, showing the cottages, the gables and the terra-cotta buildings and the cobbled streets, did nothing for my peace of mind. We followed her plan all the way—Mr. and Mrs. Walter Gotkin in town for a visit—and she led me through the streets and to the shops and stores, putting on a fine front. She laughed in public, held my hand, playing the dutiful wife and she even went with me when I shopped for some clothes on Betchnika's main drag, a street called Plotkin Boulevard. She stopped to talk to quaint village types and managed to keep me away from anything female and young that looked good in a peasant blouse and skirt. She was able to spout German, Czechoslovakian, Russian, and even a little Hungarian when it was needed. She didn't miss a bet. Only thing was she didn't realize that I could follow some of her foreign-language palaver. Especially the Russian and the German. She handled it like a pro, though. She would talk to barkeepers, shop merchants, make small talk, and idly refer to the mass lynchings. But then everybody would clam up and people would turn away, lowering their eyes and say no more. I got the distinct impression that once the formal pleasantries were over and Christina Ketch began to pry a little deeper that everyone was afraid of her; but to hear her tell it she had never been to Betchnika before, which was also odd, considering how well she knew her way around.

That was the way we spent the days—running into conversational stone walls, stopping to eat in odd little shops, and then by nightfall going back to the hotel. It was a real dead burg. Nothing went on. Even the upcoming flower festival, which was postered all over town, was going to take place about ten kilometers away at some hillside hamlet. Which figured. Betchnika's folks were slow and poky, except for some lively young peasant girls I spotted now and then as Christina Ketch steered me down the narrow cobbled streets. There wasn't much automobile traffic, either. You saw four carts or haywagons to every single car. The town was a century throwback. Like little old Germantown, New York.

The way we spent the nights was worse.

Christina always slept in the buff in the big bed next to me and I had to remind myself about our first night and her threat of castration. She didn't have to repeat her "wedding night" routine with me, because I behaved myself. Also, I was still recovering. I still felt as if I had been put through the wringer. Of course I was as Little-Big-Horny as ever, but I was smart enough to keep that to myself. I would just have to bide my time, and then—the punishment would fit the crime.

Naturally, in the evening, we would discuss the investigation. After all, we were spies on a mission. Our fact-finding project was producing nothing but goose eggs, though.

"So, Damon. You see how it is. No one wishes to discuss the lynchings. They all avoid me as soon as I mention it."

"I know. So why stall around? Why not come right out and ask them about the silver pills? And that sex orgy that went on in this town when the old men had a ball?"

"No, that is not the way. I see you are not accustomed to this sort of job. One has to be delicate and careful. Or the game will run and hide."

"If you say so. But I still think you ought to come right out and say: *What do you know about the silver pills?* What can you lose?"

"Fool!" She hissed at me in her own sweet way. "Are you forgetting what happened to the twenty-five old men? Somebody in this town murdered them. Perhaps the townspeople themselves—out of shame."

"Applesauce," I replied. "Why should they do that? I should think a real nice town would have been glad to see some old boys sowing their leftover oats. I wouldn't hang anybody for that."

"You wouldn't, but maybe Betchnika would!"

"Maybe. You still want the right side of the bed tonight?"

"Yes. It is my wish."

"Suit yourself. I'll turn out the light. Pleasant nightmares, Mrs. Gotkin."

The funny thing about that night—we slept three feet apart as usual—was that I awoke very late in the morning, feeling hung over. She was already out of the room, but I didn't care. Her company bored me, as well as frightened me. You know what it's like to be so close to a yummy broad who's nothing but bad news? My wrist was getting better and my ball zone was okay again, but I was feeling too good to risk any more bruises. I did feel groggy, though. As if I had a hangover. But I hadn't had a drop since *The King's Inn.* Betchnika had nothing but a lousy pale beer I just didn't dig. The water wasn't of the best grade, either.

With Ketch out of the way, I dashed downstairs to

try and raise Walrus-moustache on the transatlantic phone. The sleepy old desk clerk had had no luck for twenty-four hours trying to contact America. That didn't surprise me. The old telephone at the desk was a left-over from the Roaring Twenties. The clerk didn't speak anything but Czech, so I might as well have been alone.

Finally I did hook up with Walrus-moustache. His voice was faint but just as crackling and familiar as ever. He sounded very glad to hear from me. He likes me in his own pompous, thick-skinned way.

"Ah, there you are, Damon."

"Here I am. And I wish I wasn't."

"What do you mean? Has something gone wrong?"

"Nothing's right. And who is this bitch you saddled me with? Miss Ketch. B-I-T-C-H, with wheels and bells on." He laughed and I went on to expand my complaint, but he kept pooh-poohing me all the while. He just didn't know the dame, was all I could figure.

"Surely one woman can't throw you, Damon. You who have handled hundreds? Come, come, my boy, I'll wager she'll be purring like your own private kitten before the week is out."

"Wanna bet? Who the hell is she anyway?"

His voice got even lower.

"A very special agent. One of the best. All you need to know, and one of the finest career records in the organization."

"Whose organization? The Russkys?" I snarled. "Listen, give me an emergency contact here, just in case. Never can tell what might happen. Ketch and I could get separated, or just go our own ways mutually, and I'd be high and dry in this jerkwater village. Come on, now. You must have an emergency contact for me."

He grumbled. "I take it you have learned nothing in Betchnika?"

"You take it right. Everybody's dumb. Saying nothing. It happened in another part of the world. Get me? It would be smart to give me a contact here in town, who's been here awhile. He might be able to put me onto something."

"I suppose you're right. Very well. Just a moment." It took him only seconds. He must sit in front of an IBM

73

machine, wherever the hell he sits. "Katrina Walsky. The local commissar's daughter. She seems to be about twenty-two, beautiful and blonde. Rather to your prescription, I imagine. In any event, she is the contact. She is a rock and roll singer with aspirations of a Hollywood career, which is how we got her into our net. We promised to help her if she would keep her eyes and ears open in Betchnika on this silver pill thing. She may be a silly impressionable female or a very serious one. I just don't know. In any event, she does live in Betchnika and she may know something. Needless to say, her father, Commissar Walsky, knows nothing of this."

"Needless, to say. Thanks, Walrus-moustache. I'll do as much for you sometime."

"That I doubt. Really, Damon. Haven't you learned anything about this enigma?"

"Not a blessed thing. Miss Ketch is running the show. She's the bossy type. In fact, I've only learned one thing since I left America. But I shall take it with me to the grave."

"Pray what is that?"

"Never Indian hand wrestle a big-assed broad with iron hands."

"Oh. Clever. I won't ask what you mean, but I suppose it has something to do with Miss Ketch. Well, do your best, my boy. We are counting on you to solve this mystery of the pill. It's far more important than you think. Take my word for it."

"I never doubted you for a minute," I said solemnly, "but I still don't see how world peace comes into the picture. *Piece,* yes, but not *peace.*"

"You will, Damon, you will. Anything else you wished to discuss with me?"

"Yeah. Where does a guy get laid in this town?"

He snorted angrily and hung up on me. He never did appreciate my sharp sense of humor. The old mud turtle. I placed the receiver on the hook and the sleepy old clerk smiled to himself. He was still half-dozing on his feet. I shook my head, still feeling dopey from so much sleep. If I didn't know better I would have sworn somebody slipped me a Mickey. But if that was so—it could only be Christina Ketch. But why would she? All right, she was

74

bossy and officious, but she still needed me in her town-spying game. What would be the sense of putting me out of circulation? Unless she had gone to see somebody she didn't want me to see? No, it was too hare-brained and far-fetched. I'd just had a bad night's sleep. Which didn't surprise me. I was off my normal diet too. Not a broad in two whole nights. I was slipping.

Imagine the *Playboy Club* without a Bunny. In a nutshell, that is Rod Damon without some tail. Or rabbit warren.

Christina Ketch came back around noon. I was lying on the bed, doing nothing, but sunning myself and reading a copy of the *Betchnika Bugle,* which was all of six pages and just as newsworthy as the sinking of the *Titanic.* There was nothing in the dull rag to indicate anything went on in the small town. The biggest news was a runaway dog on Plotkin Boulevard. Nowhere would you have conceived that the burg had had a lynch party to top the KKK. Even on their worst nights, they never did twenty-five neckties.

"Where were you?" I asked suspiciously.

"Out."

"What did you do?"

"Nothing." That had a familiar ring. She was closed up tighter than a clam. Her usual custom at night, too. I scowled and started to light a cigarette but then I remembered her feelings about tobacco. I couldn't win for losing.

It was hard to believe she was such a bitch on wheels, looking at her. The face was a poem, the breasts an essay, and that rump deserved fifty novels at least. What a waste of girlpower!

"All right," I said, trying to make friends. "What do we do today? Should I buy you a double chocolate malted, dear Mrs. Gotkin?"

"No joking," she warned. She went to the closet and slipped off her sloppy trenchcoat. Her hips beckoned, but not to me. "Come. It is a warm day. We shall continue the investigation. There are many more shops and many more Betchnikians to see."

"You betchnika your life," I said sarcastically.

She winced. "Remember. Let me do the talking. And do stop leering at the women. The men resent it."

"Sure, sure. Anything you say."

"Then get your clothes on. I am ready. Must I stand here looking at that disgusting appendage all day?"

That was her. My girl. Christina Ketch. How could I help hating her?

So away we went, out into the cobbled streets, to talk to some more natives. I felt better though. I had an ace in the hole now. Thanks to Walrus-moustache. One Katrina Walsky, commissar's daughter. A funny thought struck me. Maybe she was a virgin too. Middle Europe seemed to be full of them, the way my luck had been going.

I didn't know what the hell Christina Ketch was.

A funny thing happened on the way to the investigation.

This time we got the real cold shoulder. I didn't have to follow all the languages to see it happening. From a word or two I knew what Christina Ketch was asking people but now they shuddered at sight of her, backed off and literally turned away from her. The same thing happened in shop after shop, on the street and in doorways when she approached townspeople. Not even the nice old ladies gave us the right time of day. We were left with egg all over our kissers. Mr. and Mrs. Walter Gotkin of West Berlin. We were, as they say in Show Biz, *dead*.

"What gives?" I asked. "You got bad breath?"

"Fool! Can't you see? They are afraid of us."

"I see. What did you ask that last old dame in the apron? She looked like she wanted to crawl into her fruit cart. I couldn't follow your Russian, you talked so fast."

"Never mind. It is enough that the woman evaded me. Come. We will go further up the street toward the end of town. More people there. For some sort of meeting." I could see the knot of gaily dressed villagers at the end of the block. But she wasn't kidding me, either. She was *evading* me too. She hadn't told me the truth about what she had asked in Russian. I was convinced of that. Miss Ketch was beginning to shape up as a bad

76

risk. If I couldn't trust her, I was really in hot water. What was her real game?

I didn't know. And when I don't know, I get nosy. Very nosy. It's the only way to stay alive.

But I followed the tall blonde up the street. She was still in charge. I pay off on my bets, and until I caught her in a real double deal, I'd play my half of the bargain. After all, I am also a man of honor. In most things outside the bedroom.

The crowd up ahead were having a kind of rally of some kind and as we drew nearer, the meeting was getting up a full head of steam. But Christina Ketch wasn't only the killjoy of *my* life. No, sir. I was now witness to one of the most amazing switcheroos in history. No sooner had we elbowed our way through the packed peasants to see what all the shouting was about than everybody suddenly froze, stopped talking, and the crowd split. I couldn't figure what happened until I realized that each of the hastily departing Betchnikians were looking back over their shoulder at us and shaking their heads fearfully. One look at the tall icy blonde and everybody all of a sudden wanted to be somewhere else. What the hell kind of whammy did she have over these simple bastards?

"All right," I said. "So it's not bad breath. What is it? These people think you're poison. I thought you said you'd never been here before. If you haven't, your twin sister sure as hell has. This crowd hates the sight of you. Or us. Which is it?"

For once, her face was drained of color. She was furious. She shook her head, snarling at me for a change. Her nostrils were flaring with rage.

"Simpletons! All of them. They are just shy of strangers. See how they run!" Run wasn't the word; they were dashing now—pouring down the street and around the corners like we had the plague or something. Dropping picnic baskets, wine bottles, flowers, the works. I haven't seen such an Exodus since the night they raided Katz's whorehouse in Racine, Wisconsin.

"I got a great idea," I said. "Let's go back to the hotel, pack and get the hell out of here. I want to go home. This silver pill jazz is a myth. And those twenty-five old guys. Must have happened in some other town. Somebody has their wires crossed."

"No," she said firmly, "it happened here, well enough. I give you my oath on that. We will simply have to try another way to get our information."

"For instance?"

"There are ways," she said stiffly. "Come. We will go back to the hotel and formulate some kind of plan. We have wasted too much time already. Something must be done and quickly."

"After you," I said, fagged out and defeated once again. She had answers and orders for everything. She must have been born saluting. All chicken, Christina Ketch. And a yard wide.

We walked all the way back to the Hotel Betchnika. We weren't that far from the place. Christina Ketch liked to walk. I didn't argue. It was a nice sunny day with no clouds, but as I expected, we got a lot of dirty looks and quickly slammed doors along the route. Not that I was suspicious of her, you understand, but I no longer trusted her any further than I could have thrown her. She hadn't leveled with me. Something was rotten in Betchnika, and I think it was Christina Ketch.

She obviously knew something I didn't, and she hadn't told me. Right then and there, walking back to that crummy hotel, I silently broke my pact with her. I didn't owe her a thing anymore. Screw her and her Indian hand wrestling matches both!

Pretending to need some cigarettes, I stopped in a drugstore along the way. She was too bored with me to follow me into the store. So I had my chance and I took it. I bought some patent medicines, had the clerk wrap them up and tucked them into my side pocket. I bought some butts too, but the medicines were a secret. You see, very few people know it, but some of the stuff that's on the market, when combined together by knowing hands, makes a very potent knockout potion. One of the things that working for the Coxemen has taught me. In fact, Walrus-moustache told me.

Turnabout was fair play. If Christina Ketch had doped me the night before last, I was about to pay her back in spades. I had some private investigating to follow up on and I didn't want her around, wide-awake, making waves. She was forever peeking over my shoulder, as it were. I wasn't going to knock her out to make love to her. That's not my speed, either.

I don't make love to clay pigeons. Only queers do.

"What took you so long?" she growled impatiently when I joined her again on the sidewalk.

"He had to break open his piggy bank to make change."

"I'm tired," she snapped. "At the hotel you will draw a bath for me and wash my back. There's no more we can do until tonight. Then we will work out a campaign of tactics."

"Okay, Boss!"

"Don't call me Boss!"

"Okay, Chief!"

"Don't call me Chief—oh, you are impossible. Why they sent me a man like you is beyond me. No wonder we aren't getting anywhere. Your intelligence is in your pants. Below your belt buckle. A man like you is doomed."

"If you say so."

"Shut up," she said wearily. I could see the attitude of the town had somehow gotten to her. Pierced the sides of the Iron Maiden. Good. I was glad. And the little surprise I had in store for her made me feel like dancing right there in the cobbled streets.

"I love you too," I said. "And I'll shut up."

I did too. All the way back to the hotel, in the elevator and up to the room, where she rapidly and efficiently undressed in her old Ninotchka way. I went into the bathroom almost gleefully, running the water, testing it with my elbow for temperature. Meanwhile, between peeks through the slitted door, I readied my homemade Mickey. It was easy. I camouflaged it all with a generous portion of red wine which the management had provided for us the day before. I filled a glass for myself and trotted out to the bedroom where she stood in all her glorious nakedness. With her back turned to me again. I felt like the second dog in a team of huskies. Only the first one ever gets a change of scenery, you know, to quote an old Hope-Crosby movie.

"Drink up," I said. "You'll feel better."

She didn't turn around. "Leave the glass in the bathroom. I'll have it in there. Forget about my back, Damon. I'll wash myself."

"Okay by me. I'm going to grab a nap. Maybe read a book."

"As you wish." As I yawned theatrically, walking toward the windows, she slithered into the bathroom, that tremendous ass rising and falling like mad. What a rump! What a shame it was attached to such a cold-hearted broad.

I lay down on the bed and waited, ear cocked to the bathroom noises. There was a pause, then a slurping sound. I was satisfied. She hadn't resisted having a belt before taking her bath. It wouldn't be long now. I started to count. Ten was the magic number. That's how fast the stuff worked, give or take a second or the constitution of the victim. In Ketch's case, I couldn't be sure of anything.

But before I silently counted to nine, there was a heavy thud of noise and a great crash of sound as if a tree had fallen. That and a liquidy *whoosh* of water splashing.

It sounded like she had made a three-point landing in the bathtub. I didn't hear the glass break, either. Maybe she still had it.

She had. You would have thought she just sat down in the tub.

And the beauty part of it was, she was so big and so naturally placed, with the bathwater just rising above her crotch, that she would wake up later on thinking she had fallen asleep in the tub. It was perfect. I shut the water taps real tight so I wouldn't drown her accidentally, took one last rueful look at the gorgeous mammaries bobbing like balloons on the gentle water, and softly withdrew.

It was high time to do some of my own snooping. I had eight hours of grace. That's how long the Mickey would take to wear off. It's plenty powerful stuff.

I wanted to make the emergency contact, in more ways than one.

Katrina Walsky, the commissar's daughter.

A rock and roll singer who wanted to go to Hollywood. Meanwhile, she spied for kicks. Okay. I'd make good use of that too if I could. The first thing I had to do was get in touch with her, though. Maybe she could tell me what the Betchnika caper was really all about. So far, for my dough, it was nothing but a gag. Something somebody dreamed up to waste the taxpayers' money. Or the Coxe Foundation's.

Either way, it would be great just talking to a real woman again. Dames like Christina Ketch could ruin you if you stayed in their company long enough. They just aren't natural.

Boy, did I miss Suzanne and Annette. And Wilhelmina. And Gretchen Zimmer. Those were the days—and the lays.

Feeling the battle call steam in my nostrils once again, I charged out of my room and flew down the stairs two at a time to the hotel lobby. I was too impatient to wait for the elevator. Not that anyone was ever using it. The Hotel Betchnika was not exactly doing an overflow business. It never would, unless the silver pills were real and were found buried somewhere in town under the cobbled streets.

The first thing I had to do was find a telephone that worked.

And call Walrus-moustache—*collect.*

CHAPTER EIGHT

Meeting Katrina Walsky was easy.

I found her home number in the Betchnika directory, called up, found out she was out, but a maidservant of some kind answered the phone and I left a message sure to draw honey. I told the maidservant to tell Miss Walsky to meet me in two hours (she was expected back soon) in the Ice Cream Parlor on Plotkin Boulevard and Swann Street. I had seen it on my travels with Christina Ketch, so it was a good enough spot to rendezvous. I was sure the Walsky kid would show up. I told the maidservant my name was Damon and I was from Hollywood, California, and I had connections with Twentieth-Century Fox. I'm dumb like a fox, sometimes.

Before the two hours were up, I did some investigating

81

of my own around town. It's funny, but without my tall blonde terror in tow, I did a helluva lot better. I didn't learn anything but nobody gave me the cold shoulder and no one ran away when they saw me coming.

After a fruitless hour of *"No"* and *"What did you say?"*, I parked myself in the Ice Cream Parlor, ordered some coffee and waited. It was a cozy little dump, with curtains, cane tables and chairs and a leitmotif of woodsiness and baroque wall paintings. The big plate glass window was comfortably curtained for semi-privacy. There were only a few customers on hand and everybody left me alone. Besides, the clothes I had bought in Betchnika were more in keeping with my surroundings. I could have been your favorite Alpine guide. Or Czech boyfriend. I had a Tyrolean hat, a tweedy sportscoat and short pants showing my nice legs. I was very much "in" for Betchnika.

Katrina Walsky showed up early. Breathless, excited, looking all around the place. I couldn't miss her. When she saw me, a face she didn't recognize, her face lit up and she came bouncing over. Whatever she was, she was the direct antithesis of Christina Ketch. She was very young, just as blonde with the ends of her long hair in two neat braids falling past her shoulders down her breasts. She was yummy, all right. Walrus-moustache had not lied. The blue skirt, tight sweater of elk-design, contained a bountifully curved shape. The skirt was mini, but Miss Walsky's legs were manifold. Strongly muscled, tanned and sexy.

"Mr. Damon?" She was chewing gum and got right to the point, sounding more American than Judy Garland in one of those old Andy Hardy movies. Her face was pure pug-nosed but wholesomely bright and attractive. Everything was there except the freckles. "I got here as quick as I could—"

"Sit down. Want an ice cream soda?"

Her nose wrinkled. "Who can eat ice cream at a time like this? Say, if you're really from Hollywood and Fox can it be because you heard some of the demos I cu with Roland's Right-hand Men and maybe want to ar range a screen test?"

I had to smile. "Sorry. Not this trip. But we will follow

82

through on you, I promise. Fact is, I'm a Coxeman and I was told to contact you about the Betchnika lynchings." My voice fell to a whisper, but it didn't fall as far as her smile did. She slumped back in her chair and her twin, nicely pointed breasts poked out at me almost accusingly.

"Oh—that old thing. Damn, I knew it was too good to be true. So you're not from Hollywood."

"Sorry, but I have been instructed to tell you that the people you talked to are trying to arrange a test for you. I hear you have a great voice. Like Garland." What harm could little white lies do?

She brightened immediately. "Really? 'Course I'm not as good as Judy. Or Streisand, either. I'm more in Nancy Sinatra's class."

"Think big. Why not aim higher? Anyhow, we must get right down to business, Miss Walsky. You know how dangerous this all is—"

"Call me Katie. Everybody does. What's your first name? You're cute."

"Rod. Like in McKuen." She liked that too. I felt better already. She seemed a smart, perky gal and we ought to have a few laughs together before all this madness was done. "Now what about those lynchings and this silver pill business. The people who said they'd send you to Hollywood would be damn grateful if you've come up with anything."

She smiled. "Oh, I have. I know where the laboratory is. What they're doing. Everything."

I stared at her. "You do?"

"Sure. Poppa may be a Communist tool, but I'm not. I don't like Pops much. He used to beat my mother up. And then she died. So I don't care what I do to get him into trouble. See how it is?"

"I see." I looked around. We were almost alone. Nobody was close enough to hear us. And the counter people were all busy doing their thing. "Then please tell me what you know without further delay. The Coxemen are anxious to get moving on this thing."

"Not as anxious as I am to hit L.A. Gee, do they really have all those swimming pools and oranges?"

"Tons. Now about these lynchings—"

She made a face. "That was an experiment. You see,

83

out at the Firnl Lab they were making tests. They came up with this pill. You just swallow it and zowie—you're a kid again, and you can make love for hours. So they tried it out on the old men, twenty-five of them. I guess you know what happened. The old geezers turned the town upside down. The women were begging them for it. And then the men who didn't get pills got mad and—well, one morning, the poor old fellows were found strung up. Lots of people think the jealous men did it. I don't. I know who did it. An executioner for the MVD. Those bastards! Ugh. Anyhow—nothing's happened since. You see, new experiments are going on all the time at Firnl. They haven't perfected the thing yet."

"How come you know all this?"

She shrugged. "Poppa. The big domes from Moscow come to our house to set up their projects and things. This is still a Red satellite, you know. No matter how they spell it out."

She was a literal gold mine of information. I reached across and squeezed her hand. She squeezed back. For all her rapid-fire, big-girl spiel, she blushed and her breasts jumped. I filed the view for future study.

"What about the new experiments? Can you tell me anything about that?" She nodded and brushed a braid away from one of her whim-whams.

"Sure. Two Russian doctors at Firnl—Gekko and Or-koff—have come up with a solution to the pill's bugs. You see, the pill is a fooler. Just the right amount of chemicals must go into each pill to match the metabolism of each man who gets it. You see? A man with low blood pressure, for instance, or high blood pressure, could die, otherwise. The pills contain strychnine, which you oughta know is a well-known but very dangerous aphrodisiac. So Gekko and Orkoff have the job of standardizing the pill. That's why they had the tests with the old men. And more are coming. Mark my words."

"You found all this out at your house?"

"Sure. Gekko and Orkoff always come for a glass of beer and discuss their plans with Poppa. They bring their attaché cases with them and leave them lying around. I can read."

84

"I'll say you can. It's probably highly technical data. How come you can translate it?"

"Majored in Biology at Prague University and then I had to come back to this crummy town to die on the vine. Still, there's hope. I *can* sing. Wanta hear me do 'These Shoes Were Made For Walking'?"

"Later. I promise you. If you're free today I want you to come to my hotel."

"Yeah?" Her eyes shone. "You like me? I like you."

"Yes, I like you. More than you know. And we'll talk about that later too. Honest. But I want you to meet my partner, and then I want you to take us out to that barn where the old men were hanged. We might pick up another lead."

Her face fell. "Your partner?"

"Don't worry your head about her. She's a cold fish who wouldn't wipe her shoes on me. And vice versa. You want me, baby, you got me. But business first. And I do want to call in all this valuable dope you've given me. One thing more—are you a virgin?"

She grinned at me. "Is it important?"

"No. Just curious."

"Then the answer is—find out for yourself."

"Okay, I will. Come on. Time's a-wasting. The sooner we close today's investigation, the sooner I can find out. Okay?"

"Okay!" She stood up. Bright, bouncing, and just bubbling over with good will and warmth and cooperation. I'd made a big score. "You really are an American, Rod. No boy in this town would ever talk the way you do."

"Don't give me that. You can't be the average Betchnikian maid, either."

"I'm not," she laughed. "How'd you guess?"

"It's your eyes. Each one of your baby blues has a great big *Yes* in them."

"Then don't say No," she challenged. "Where's your hotel?"

"The *Betchnika*. Are there others?"

"A couple more. That's no worse than the rest of them. Tell me. Are you really just a spy, Rod? Man like you. Bet you're something real special."

"How can you tell?"

85

"Your flashlight is showing and I never met any man who stuck out the way you do." Laughing, she jabbed me in the ribs playfully and went tripping ahead of me to wait at the door while I paid the bill. Grinning to myself, and a little red-faced, I coughed as I fumbled for some change. Didn't I tell you I was hurting? Normally, I can exercise great control, but Christina Ketch had imposed a starvation diet on me and I was as loose as a goose and twice as ready for plucking.

Katrina Walsky took my arm on the sidewalk and smiled up at me. That was another thing I liked about her. She was more like five feet five, instead of an Amazon. But there wasn't a small thing on her. She exuded radiance and sex appeal by the yard.

"You like to screw, Rod?" She said it softly, almost reverently. Again, my kind of girl.

"You said it."

"That's nice," she murmured and snuggled up next to me, her head lolling against my shoulder as we strolled back to the hotel. I wondered how she would react to sight of Christina Ketch. That damn female brought out the worst in everybody.

Still, even on such short notice, I would bet my money on Katrina Walsky.

Katie.

She had rock and she had roll.

I intended to put both talents to great use.

Christina Ketch was still slumbering peacefully in the bathroom when we slunk in. Some four hours had elapsed of the eight-hour grace period for the duration of the Mickey Finn. Nothing had changed. Ketch hadn't moved a muscle. Her large breasts slumped placidly in the cold bathwater, bobbing like toy balloons. The sleepy downstairs clerk hadn't batted an orb when I marched in with Katrina Walsky. Nor even heard Katie singing a soft and low rock and roll number. The girl was happy, for some reason other than being young, alive and full of beans. I guess she really liked me.

But she didn't like Christina Ketch.

No sooner had she stopped to stare down at the sleeping Amazon in the tub than her face fell again, lost color and something fierce and guttural like the Czechoslovakian version of *"Drop Dead!"* shot out of her. Worse than that, though, and far more baffling, Katie's face froze into a mask of hatred, she took a step forward and spit into the tub. A real oyster. I grabbed her by the arm.

"Jealous, already? Hold on. She doesn't mean a thing to me but bad news."

"You dummy!" Katie roared, whirling on me, jabbing me savagely in the chest with her forefinger. "That's your partner? Her? *Him!* You poor sap—that's Chris!"

"Sure it is. Christina Ketch. She was sicked onto me by my employers as a fellow agent. She is no pal, though. What do you mean—*him?*"

A great light went on in my brain.

Katie was close to tears. "Rod, Rod. That's the MVD executioner! The one who killed the old men. Don't you see?"

I stood there, baffled.

Angrily, defiantly, Katie bent down and pulled the stopper out of the tub. The water gurgled and began to flow out. Slowly, and then very rapidly. I blinked and all the time Katie was blurting out the news of the day. For a second, I just couldn't think straight. It was all happening too fast.

"Chris is a top executioner, Rod. A man, not a woman. Never mind those breasts. That's silicone treatments. All padding. Same for the hips and rump. You'll see when the water goes down. This is a pretty boy who can go drag now and then for reasons of espionage but she's— he's a man, all the same. Probably wants to be one more than anything. Look—for the love of Betchnika—see for yourself now!"

I saw all right. The glory mound was there. All scraggly from the bath now and clinging. But it couldn't hide the penis, no bigger than a peanut, nestling among the foliage. Chris, or Christina Ketch, or whoever the hell he or she was, just hadn't had the rubles to go to Denmark for the Jorgenson special yet. Ouch. I felt sick. I sat down on the john seat and shook my head.

Katie was breathing funny.

"Look at him. He put the ropes around those poor old necks and sprung the traps. All by himself. What an awful person! He's better off dead. We should kill joy-fully—"

She didn't sound like a rollicking young woman who wanted to go to Hollywood anymore. She sounded like a dedicated executioner.

"His name is Chris—?" It was all I could say just then. I was thinking about a lot of things.

"Yes. Just Chris. Probably a short version of Chrisofsky or something. I don't blame you for not knowing it was a man. Look at the face. It does belong on a woman. Those cheekbones, that mouth—"

She rambled on, low-voiced and angry, and I was still thinking of all the things that had confused and hurt me the last three days.

Like losing at Indian hand wrestling.

Like getting pushed around in my own bed.

Like not being wanted by Christina Ketch, who had the guts to dare sleep naked with me in the dark.

Who didn't mind my seeing her backside when she undressed. What a laugh. A man all the time.

Also, some other vital things.

Like the people of Betchnika running and hiding every time they saw us coming. They must have recognized him——her after a time and that was too much for them. There wasn't anything they could do about Chris's return to the scene of the crime but they didn't have to like it. They hadn't.

It was easy to my male ego and pride to tell myself that Christina Ketch had Lesbian tendencies or was a cold fish—that part I could have believed—but to have her turn out a *man* was too much. I should have known. I should have guessed. Me, Rod Damon, who could recognize fifty different women in total darkness.

Obviously there were still some avenues of sexology I still had to research. Chris couldn't be that good an actor to totally disguise his masculine origin, no matter what the odds. I had slipped up somewhere. In my vanity, I hadn't even sensed the basic difference in the genders that should have told me that Chris was a man and not a woman. That was an error totally inconsistent with my training and experience. I was ashamed of myself.

I went into the bedroom, dug Chris's wicker suitcase

out of the closet and ransacked it. The feminine finery was a mockery now. But there was nothing in the suitcase to hook the man-woman in the tub up with MVD or anything subversive. There wasn't even a weapon of any kind.

Katie had followed me from the bathroom.

"What are you going to do about Chris?"

"The smartest thing I ever did was looking you up, Katie. I think our MVD character would have fooled me until he killed me."

"Well, he can't do that now." I had explained to her on the way to the hotel about the Mickey and the suspicions I had. "At least you suspected something. That says a lot."

"Maybe."

"If you're in doubt, just remember this bastard killed twenty-five old men. Without batting an eye—same way you ordered your coffee in that ice cream parlor."

"You're right."

"Also he's the enemy. One of *them*. We don't do something about it, we may never get another chance like this."

"Uh huh."

"You reading me right, Rod?"

"I am." I smiled at her. "Where did you say that barn was?"

She threw her arms around my neck, hugged me, planted a big kiss on my mouth and gyrated her hips to show me how real she was. She ground her chest into me. Her eyes misted.

"Don't worry about me. I'm female, all right. Too much so, maybe. But right now, you follow me. We'll unload Chris and then come back here. Okay?"

"Deal. I want to reaffirm my faith in womankind."

She nodded and skipped back into the bathroom, taking the measure of the sleeping killer in the tub. It was still so hard to believe. Every woman should be built the way this executioner was!

"God, he's a big one! But we can manage somehow—"

Darkness was coming on so that made things a lot easier. The sleepy clerk downstairs hardly saw us as we bundled Chris out to the Renault. Katie drove and I kept Chris under wraps in the back seat. I had redressed him-her, in the sloppy trenchcoat, and that was all. He-she was still sleeping off the drug. It was just as well. I'm not that cold-blooded even if the punishment was going to fit the crime.

Katie was a wild, reckless driver, but somehow she managed to get us out to the famous barn in less than half an hour. It was somewhere in the forest beyond town. A great, rambling, empty, dilapidated structure where you could still hear the rats scurrying around. There was a wide, thick central beam that ran across the very heart of the place. We had lashed Chris's hands behind him and found a rickety chair in the barn. It had probably served the same purpose before. I stood Chris on this while Katie looped a clothesline around his neck and slung it over the central beam. The ghosts of twenty-five old geezers might have been chuckling, the way the evening breezes whipped through the barren, rickety barn. I retied Chris's hands in the front.

When we had Chris dangling so that his feet still rested on the chair, I arranged the chair so that the slightest struggle on his part would kick the thing over and all of his great weight would drop down, suspended a good two feet from the floor. Just enough to break his murderous neck and hang him. Same way he had done the old men.

We had found the clothesline still in the barn. That too was somehow poetic justice. I had no qualms about arranging an MVD man's death. He had it coming all right, and as Katie said, it was him-her or us.

But I couldn't bring myself to pen the few lines that would tell the world and Betchnika exactly why an MVD man had taken his own life in the very same barn where he had executed so many nice old guys.

FOR WHAT I DID TO THE OLD
MEN OF BETCHNIKA, I AM TRULY
SORRY. GOD SAVE ME.
                                CHRIS.

Katie wrote the suicide note, with all the glee and fervor she might have felt writing a fan letter to Frank Sinatra. That girl was all heart.

Finally the deed was done.

We drove back to the hotel in the Renault. More slowly this time. Katie was smiling with grim satisfaction.

"What's so funny?" I wanted to know.

"That barn. I wish we could have waited around until he woke up, kicked the chair over and got his neck stretched. What a sight to see—"

"I can skip it, thank you." The night was cold and never in my life have I so much wanted to hop into bed with a good woman. Katie was in for it, whether she wanted it or not.

"Rod."

"Yes?"

"Still want me, like you said?"

I laughed. "Katie, you try to chicken out on me now, I swear you'll wind up with two broken legs and no teeth. That answer your question?"

"Yipppeeeee!" she yelled. "Tonight's the night!" The Renault shot forward like a lightning bolt. I smiled to myself. I wouldn't take any bets but I smelled a virgin again. Maybe she talked tough and jazzy, but I detected another green olive in my vicinity.

I didn't mind.

Dealey was high on virgins when he was alive and I told you what I think of them. They are still the experience of any man's lifetime, if he handles it right. So help me, Jalal al-Din al-Siyuti!

And girls are something I have always known how to handle. All kinds of girls. Queers like Christina Ketch-Chris are something else again. They give me the creeps.

The Katies of this world are more in my province.

You can take the spy racket. And world peace and silver pills and all that gook.

Without a dame, it doesn't mean a row of petunias.

We got back to the Hotel Betchnika in fifteen minutes flat. Night had shut down the town. The fireflies were glowing again.

We got upstairs and undressed in another five.

Five minutes later, Katie came to me.

I came to her.

And after that, we just came and went all night.

She was a virgin, all right, but the kind of virgin of your wildest fancies.

Ready, willing and able to try anything.

And as trusting as a young woman can be.

For the first time in three days, I was doing what came naturally for Rod Damon. I'm not ashamed to admit I went whole hog. I had a lot of catching up to do.

Pardon me while I indulge myself with a blow-by-blow account of the oldest ball game in the universe.

I had grown horns where I never had them before. The steam was charging out of my nostrils; I was pawing the ground like a horse in the mating season; I was huffing and puffing for all I was worth.

And I had Katie. Dear little Katrina Walsky.

What a far cry from Ice Cold Christina!

She was only a commissar's daughter, but she didn't need any commissaring.

Czech and double-Czech!

I was going to make her forget all about *Roland's Right-hand Men*. I had a combo she had never come up against before. She couldn't have. She might not know the lyrics, but all I had to do was hum a few bars and she'd be toddlin' along with Rod.

I have that Hit Parade all to myself and the Top Ten would take a backseat to me.

Damon and Double-Damon!

CHAPTER NINE

I stripped.

She stripped.

Then we approached each other from both sides of the bed. Warily, taking each other's measure. Her's were fine. About 36x22x36, all packed on that five-foot-five frame of delectable flesh. She was a finely different kind of virgin. Not at all scared, no stammers, no gulps. She knew what she wanted and she was going to get it.

She took my measure too. I'd left a small lamp burning by the bed, so she could find her way to all the important things. Her blue eyes goggled, but she didn't retreat. In fact, she couldn't take her eyes off it once she saw it.

Even as she lay down on the big soft bed waiting for me to deliver the bacon, she was mesmerized at the sight. Her mouth moistened, her breasts tautened into live things and her arched hips moved sinuously on the coverlet. Hollywood! She must have seen all the sex movies that were ever made. She had a wiggle and a slither right out of an avant garde film.

I got on the bed and straddled her, standing above her and looking down. I'd decided to skip all the expertise, the foreign erotica, the age-old customs and mores. This called for straight-on-tactics, a real drop-and-plunge hell-for-leather bang. I intended to be gentle. But I'd had the Great Stone Ache for days now and I needed ash-hauling badly. She could see I did. I looked like I was mooring the *Hindenburg*.

"Oh, Rod," she said huskily, looking up at me and mine. "Are you for real? Or do you wind that thing with a crank from the side?"

"No jokes, please. You like it?"

"Silly man." She reached up, got two handholds and wriggled her fingers. "Do we choose up sides?"

"Not necessary. I know whose side you're on." I stared down at the fulsome convex of her thighs. She was prime. Real tenderloin. Even her pubic garden looked fresh and untouched by human hands. I began to lower myself. Now, she did gasp and her hands fanned out, palming my undercarriage and jiggling the two wheels. Her eyes rolled and closed like shutters.

"I knew this day would come," she breathed low. "I wanted to pick the spot—I picked you. Now you pick a spot and go, man, go! The suspense is killing me. Can I be able to take a thing that size?"

"You'd be surprised. First, two questions. No, three."

Her eyes popped up and open. She looked disappointed.

"Questions? You're kidding—"

"No, I am not. Now, do you consider this a rude object?"

"Only if you don't slam it into me first chance you get!"

"Good. Now, do you think it is a disgusting appendage?"

93

"No, no—it's the most beautiful thing I've ever seen. I swear on all my rock and roll records. Including my Tom Jones albums."

"Last but not least—am I a freak?"

"Vive la freaks—" she muttered weakly, biting her lip, beginning to shake with expectation. I nodded happily. She had told me all I wanted to know. I tell you— that Ketch broad had gotten under my skin.

So I lowered away.

Slowly, just letting about two inches of hot steel touch Katie. She moaned, caught her breath and with a wisdom beyond her experience, simply widened the V of her cream-colored thighs. Then she began to rock and roll. Gently, not wildly. Her own desires and natural lubricity began to widen the orifice. For me, she was the balm of the ages. I felt anointed with oils. I slipped in another inch or so. She parted the gates of Eden and kept on widening. With slow, careful precision until it was very easy for me to drop the rest of the way. Not the *Damon Drop*—it was far too early for that. I would have ruined her forever. Nay, I merely slid all the way home without pushing too hard and in no time at all she had locked me in her furry prison and thrown the key away. I had sized her up correctly. An impatient virgin, a bold one, and certainly not the kind to bleat at the first twinges of pain. But Katie knew herself better than I did. Very soon, she had wrapped herself around the joystick and me with all the fervor and yearning of a woman who has waited. Once she had me tight, she never let go.

All I had to do was man the pumps.

Her deflowering was exquisite. It lasted a helluva lot longer than many another First Time. Katie knew how to give and take. The best combination in the world for a woman getting her boots laced and her ribbons pulled.

We rolled, writhed and copulated with stunning ease. The bed was large and roomy, and for each cold night I had endured with Christina Ketch, I redoubled my stroke. But finally, inevitably, Katie weakly had to call for Time. There wasn't a patch of her warm flesh that wasn't wet. Her splendid mammaries were as hard as coconuts now and the muscles of her thighs and hips curled and arched with trembling release. Speaking for

94

myself, I was ten pounds lighter, fit as a bull fiddle and ready for more. But the first necessary madness had been excellently served and now I could finesse the rest of the night away. Katie wasn't going anyplace.

She sprawled across my chest, her hands still clutching the family jewels, plaiting the separate hairs the same way she must have done her long golden hair. Her hilly rump, round and firm and fully packed, blotted out the view of the lousy wallpaper of the room. Outside, the town of Betchnika slept. It was very late in the day. Not so much as a car horn squalled.

I hadn't subsided, of course, and to Katie this was a marvel without equal.

She muttered something in Czechoslovakian that sounded like awe and I chuckled. She answered that by gently squeezing my testicles. All that did was make the topmost tower stretch an inch further.

"What do I need to make that go down, Rod? Beat it with a stick?"

"I stay ready," I said. "You complaining?"

"Oh, Rod." She smothered it with kisses, rising to her knees to snuggle. Her mouth was one hot little item. I stirred pleasurably.

"You're not as pure as the driven snow anymore," I reminded her. "Mind very much?"

"So I drifted." She sat back on her haunches and I could see the gleam of her eyes and the tender shadows her breasts threw even in the dim light. "When I think of the years I wasted—but not even Karl Orlonikek was as big as you are!"

"Who he?"

"Just a boy who used to take me dancing. We'd pet on the porch until Poppa caught us. He never came back. Folks are afraid of commissars around here, you know."

"How big was Karl?"

She chuckled. "You men. Always wanting to know if you're bigger than the next one!" I told you she was a hep chick. "Well, you are. Let's put it this way, if we were talking about tobacco, he'd be a cigarette and you'd be a cigar."

I teased her. "Want to smoke, Katie?"

"Oh, can I? May I? I wondered if you'd let me—"

She crouched forward and I felt marvelous. "I didn't know if you approved of such things!" Her tongue flicked out like a darting snake.

"When it comes to men and women, I don't draw the line at sexual limits. Be my guest. Enjoy. Later on, I'll give you some lip service you may remember all your born days."

She didn't need any urging.

She began to lick away, eating from the top down, and before she or I knew what was happening, she'd traveled all the way to the danger line and almost mechanically now, without asking, she hoisted herself atop me once more. And again we were off to the races. This time I ploughed into her at Yankowski's fabulous forty-five-degree angle until she was moaning for me to stop, then I turned her over on her stomach and the ancient Greek Art of the Back-Scuttle has seldom known such zealous championing. But I hadn't pegged her wrongly at all. Even in that rather helpless position, she was able to rock and roll back into me until I had to triple my stroke to keep her from mashing me backwards. Following which gainful employment, we immediately reversed roles and she tried to do me from the top. But there I really had her. And in less time than it takes to shake a joystick, she soon collapsed atop the flagpole, tired and spent. All in all, we had been busy a good two hours, and Katie Walsky had sampled a little of everything that is, at least, natively Damon and basically American. The Greeks don't exactly do it the way we do—but that's another story.

I carried her into the bathroom, set her down in the tub and let some warm water revive her. She drowsed sleepily, her breasts still pulsating. The refreshing bath made her perk up. She stared up at me with love and wonder in each eyeball. And still I hadn't really gone down. I rode proudly in the range of her vision.

"Good God," she murmured.

"Thank God," I said.

"I used to think singing was everything, but you opened my eyes. Belting out ballads and tunes just can't compare to this. What a shame it can't be waxed and sold as a record label."

"Please. The mere idea makes me sick. You okay?"

"If I was a kitten, I'd meow and howl off the back fence."

"But you are pussy. Prime pussy, believe me. For a newcomer to this art, you're kind of fabulous yourself. You're going to have a long and fruitful life, Katie."

"Is that a promise?"

"On my oath."

"Climb in. You wash too. I'll do your back. I hope that fiend Chris has kicked over the chair. Hanging's too good for him."

I got in the tub and she made room. We locked into a beautiful pretzel formation that still left us face to face. She was warm and so good to look at. I fondled her chest fondly. She sighed and arched her shoulders in another V.

"Mmmmmmm," she said. "Do that again."

"I can and will, ma'am."

"You know something? I wouldn't have believed it. But I'll be raring to go again in a minute—"

"Rare away. There's no law against it."

She nodded happily, took the bar of soap and scrubbed away at my deltoids, rib cage and back. I returned the compliment. She grinned and fidgeted. The fever was returning, and like she had said, that was new to her too. But she was so willing to learn. The perfect pupil.

"Rod. You have to stay on this silver pill case?"

"Sure, it's my job. Why?"

She shrugged. "Nothing. Just that you ought to know everything. The Firnl Lab is about three miles from here and a couple of miles from there is a small Skoda works, a cannon section. You ought to know that the women who work there have been hanging around the lab when they finish their shifts. Every day. Like clockwork."

"What for?"

"Rumors are around about the pills. Everybody remembers about the old men and what happened. So these women hang around waiting for some of the studs to come out—you know, men who might have been dosed with the pill. You know how women are. Like lunatics when it comes to a good man in bed. Especially, a super-charged man. Thought I ought to tell you. You might think of something."

"I already have. Let's dry off and go back to bed. Good thing you told me, Katie. This could be important."

"Not as important as what you've got," she pouted. "You don't need silver pills. You're a giant!"

"Don't lose your head, now."

We toweled each other down and she shivered ecstatically. I could see she was all gingery and ready to go again. It's great to be young, isn't it? No tired blood, no need for silver pills. Just your youth, your dreams and a lot of get up and go and you're all set. You don't have to get Life out of any bottles or wonder drugs. Or new inventions.

By the time we reached the bed, I had a plan half-formed. Sure. It made sense. Hang around that Firnl Lab, pretend to be one of the sexed-up males, grab some of the horny, desperate females and in return for some loving, they might tell all they knew. Hell, they must have seen something or knew something at least, hanging around the Lab like that, everyday. It was worth trying.

When I detailed my plan to Katie, she grudgingly admitted it was a fair scheme that might work. But I could see she didn't like the idea too much of sharing her claim with anyone else. Still, she was a game trouper and did understand the vicissitudes of espionage. It was like a That's-Show-Biz! situation.

"Never mind, Katie. You can help. And I can promise you there'll always be a lamp burning for you in my fly. Scout's honor."

"You're no Boy Scout. You're a Wolf Pack leader."

"So I am." I slipped my hand between her legs and she sighed helplessly and began to twitch again. She was like me. Always ready. I wished I had her back at the university to help me out with my Masters-Johnson tests. Her response factor was hypersensitive. "And what are you, my girl?"

"Your horny little, ever-loving, always-wanting woman! Oh, Rod—I feel it again—it's coming over me like a tide. Is it always like this?" She let out a shriek of delight. A low cry as the lightning touched her rod. She quivered electrically; shot sparks and the current flowed. I put her

98

legs up past my shoulders and raised my body. Her eyes opened; fear almost came into them; the *Damon Drop* can be frightening to a newcomer, even if it is a special girl like Katie Walsky. She knew I wouldn't hurt her; she just didn't know how much she could take. I knew, though. She was now ready. Her snatch was made for plummeting. The higher the better, the deeper the greater. She was still bottomless and she didn't know that, either.

"Oh, oh—what are you doing—oh, that smarts!"

"Just a second longer. And then it won't. Today you are a woman. This is your diploma, Katrina Walsky."

"Is it? What did I do?"

"You were a woman when you walked into this room and you have remained a woman ever since."

"Then"—she gasped, straining as her warm thighs passed to their full length above my shoulders—"sock it to me!"

On the words, I dropped from the ceiling. It's my own ploy, my own baby, my own little invention and as I like to repeat has won the day all over the world.

Like so many women before her, and I hope ever after, and like Gretchen Zimmer of Munich, Katie Walsky did the only thing likely and possible under the imposed circumstances and positions of our bodies.

Her shapely body gave one galvanic twitch, she struggled to come erect, her thighs seemed to wave like flags, she cried out with a mighty moan of ecstasy—and fainted.

Flat on her back, dead away.

After all, she was only a virgin. Correction. Had been.

And now, as I had told her, she was really a woman.

She had given me everything I wanted plus the extra little thing that was necessary to my stay in Betchnika. I now knew what my next move was in Operation Silver Pill.

The Firnl Laboratory near the Skoda works, Cannon Section.

Where hungry women waited and lusted after ingested studs.

Exactly my speed.

That kind of investigation was the sort of thing that was right up my alley. All the way up.

Katie slept blissfully on the bed as I lay back, smoking

99

a cigarette and planning tomorrow's strategy. She breathed deeply and it was nice watching her yum-yums rise and fall. What a girl.

I was terribly fond of her already.

And if I had anything to say about it, I would see that she got her crack at the Big Apple—star time U.S.A.

I owed her that much for being such a sport about everything.

Besides, I was still going to need her help if I ever wanted to keep my record even at 1000—I'd run up that kind of batting average working for Walrus-moustache and the Coxe Foundation. I hadn't missed yet.

Now that I'd separated myself from the questionable aid of one Christina Ketch, I had to have a partner, didn't I? What better help could I get than a native-born Betchnikian with a nice wiggle and a willingness to learn from the great Damon?

You said it, boys and girls.

I'd found my real ally for the silver pill caper.

Katrina Walsky, Girl Guide.

K-K-K-Katie!

CHAPTER TEN

The next day we stayed in the hotel. I was waiting for night to fall so we could go out to the Firnl Laboratory and try my plan. There was a little radio in the room, a powerful five-watter that sort of gave out the local news. I ordered our meals from the sleepy clerk downstairs. Katie did go out once, to check in at her home and make it look like she'd been home all night, and then she came back right away. It seemed that Poppa commissar left her pretty much to her own devices. So much for motherless kids. Anyhow, Katie, when she came back breathlessly with eyes shining (the mere idea of being alone with a lover in a hotel room all day was a drug to her) reported that Poppa Walsky was hip-deep in conference with Gekko and Orkoff again. The Firnl Lab scientists had some fresh data of a sort. Katie couldn't tell what but it didn't matter.

While we ate our bread, cheese and wine, I kept my

ears tuned to the radio. Along about two o'clock, the Czech-spouting newscaster announced the death of Chris in the barn. Katie translated for me. The announcer sounded like he was doing a weather report but I got all the details anyway. Betchnika Radio made no comment on the death except to mention the suicide note without revealing its contents or making any reference to the murders of the twenty-five old men. That figured. It was still a Communist station, no matter how you sliced it, and no matter how small the town of Betchnika was. Maybe that's why Moscow had chosen such an isolated little burg to conduct their experiments in the first place. It added up.

Between eating and listening to the radio, Katie and I made love again. Sometimes she was the aggressor. Sometimes I was. It's nice to have a healthy once-was virgin around a hotel room. Especially on rainy days. I was glad about the rain. It fit in with my little scheme for the Firnl Lab like I fit into Katie. But she never did stop marveling at my incredible build and indefatigable desire to fornicate.

Time humped on and we were both happy. We took about three baths apiece, renewed ourselves, and refreshed our bodies. Toward five o'clock, I was ready for my work in the field. Katie got her clothes back on almost ruefully. I'd found out a lot about her in a short time. She had the makings of a female Rod Damon. She knew what she had, how to use it, and never tired of variety or degree of performance. I was thoroughly pleased with her. Hollywood didn't know what it was missing.

"What time does that Skoda factory close?" I asked. "I want to be at the Firnl when those women are hanging around."

"Five o'clock. Skoda has a strong union. Same as everybody else." She sighed, looking at the bed, the sheets, the battered pillows, the lousy wallpaper of the room. She rubbed her stomach tenderly.

She looked like she was going to cry.

"What's the matter, Katie?"

"I'm going to miss this room. Just because it was my first illicit experience. My very first *experience*. It's like my honeymoon suite."

"Cut that out. You'll see a thousand rooms and a thousand experiences before you cash in your chips. Besides, we'll come back here and I'll roll you over and do it all over again."

"Promise. Cross your heart and hope to die?"

"I'll promise but I never hope to die."

"You wouldn't," she agreed almost ruefully. "You've got too much to live for."

"Pot calling the kettle black." I pushed her toward the door. "Come on. Show me these hungry, yearning women, aching to be raped."

It was raining cats and dogs when we reached the street. We had to race to the Renault. I let Katie drive again. The skies were dark and rumbling thunder rolled in the heavens. Then a jagged flash of lightning ripped across the firmament. That was perfect. I hope it kept up until we reached the Firnl Lab. I wondered how Chris was doing at the local morgue.

"Rod," Katie murmured, as she sped the Renault along the cobbles, taking the main drag out of town, "you do like me just a little, don't you? I mean—oh, damn!"

"Sure, baby. Just remember that whatever I do in the next few hours is all for the cause. I'm a dedicated man. It's part of the job."

She didn't say anymore, gave the Renault some gas and we climbed out of town, leaving the gables, the terracotta and the chimneys behind us. In the teeming rain, Betchnika looked more like a ghost town than ever.

It *wasn't* a nice place to visit and I *wouldn't* want to live there.

Nobody would. Even if it was the place Katrina Walsky hung up her bra and panties.

The Firnl Lab was a square, stone, tomb of a building set down in a clearing, sheltered on all four sides by tall elms and spruces. In the sheets of rain and occasional flashes of lightning, it looked awesome and unfriendly. Katie knew exactly what to do. She slithered the Renault to a stop on the curving macadam roadway leading up to the building and parked about a hundred feet before the entrance. The car was hidden by a leafy bower of forsythia and a high hedge of privets. I peered through

102

the windshield. The front of the building looked unguarded and unprotected. High windows with thick pebbled glass hid any view of what was going on within those low four walls. Off to the left, a towering smokestack stretched into the sky. No smoke was issuing from its mouth. A phallic symbol of sorts—if there ever was one. If this was the true home of silver pills, it was a great advertisement.

"So where're the hungry broads?" I asked.

Katie snorted. "You blind? Look!"

I looked. Near the huge steel doors that fronted the facade, I could see now a low stone patio with an iron railing. Standing there, huddled like churchgoers near a shrine, were about eight women, all ulstered and macintoshed and umbrella-ed. The women were heedless of the downpouring rain. All of their attention seemed to be riveted on the big main doors and another exit cut out in the face of the building about twenty feet to the right. That, too, fit my plan to a T. I eased out of the Renault. Katie jumped.

"Where are you going?"

"Step One, silly. Remember? Now, you're sure about that other abandoned storehouse nearby? We'll need it if this works."

She nodded. "I told you. When you come out of the buildings, bear left through that break in the trees. There's a bad road. Never used. Keep on going for about a hundred yards and you can't miss it. What will you do if they catch you before you make the storehouse?"

"I'll worry about that when the time comes. Now, you wait like you promised. Then meet me at the storehouse. I'll need you like crazy if none of these dames talks English."

Again, she nodded, worried. "All right. I hope you know what you're doing."

"I hope I know what I'm screwing, is what you mean."

With that, I dashed from the car. The rain pelted me and the lightning flashed again. Making good time and no noise, nothing that could be heard in such a downpour, I gained the cut-out exit to the right of the main entrance of the Firnl Lab. It worked like a charm. None of the waiting dames had seen me. I peeked out. There was something comic and forlorn, the way they stood around silently, waiting for the human guinea pigs to come out. I had to work fast before one of them did emerge from the building. That would just about ruin everything.

It all depended on the lightning. And the thunder.

I waited, praying, and then a rolling, rumbling roar of heavenly noise echoed overhead. Right on its heels, came the flashing, blinding burst of lightning. Quickly, I sprang from the concealment of the doorway and began walking nonchalantly from the building. I got about ten feet before the women spotted me. As I had calculated, temporarily blinded by the lightning flash, it looked for all the world as if I had just come from the building. That was all those broads needed.

A great, unified feminine shout of triumph went up. I looked back. I recoiled. The eight broads had left the patio and were swooping like a tide toward me, ulsters flopping, umbrellas waving like swords. I couldn't see their faces. But there was no mistaking their intent. Their hands were extended like claws—that purely open gesture of *"Gimme! Gimme! Gimme!"* or *"Mine! Mine! Mine!"* I lowered my head and ran. In the opposite direction. Toward the break in the trees and that bad road that led down to an abandoned storehouse. I needed the whole setup for my plan to work.

I'm a fine runner, I starred at track in college, but I'm telling you, those eight hungry women were breathing down my neck by the time I staggered off the road into full view of that ramshackle building. I could smell them, hear them, yammering and shouting behind me. Even in a medley of rain noises. I pounded up to the front door of the storehouse, and turned. Was I glad to see Katie's Renault chugging into the small areaway behind me! But the oncoming tide of females ignored the car and kept on coming. Shuddering, I dashed inside the building, feeling like a drowned rat. The place was almost a duplicate of the barn where we had left Chris to his own devices. But it was dry and comfortable. Still, I couldn't help feeling trapped. If the eight women were really hostile, I could be torn limb from limb. What if they had been *without it* for days?

I backed away in the interior, eyes on the door. Ready. Waiting. It was now or never. I could hear them fumbling at the wooden barrier.

They galloped in, slamming the rickety door open, and suddenly I was face to face with eight women. Eight yearning, sex-crazed females. I looked at them. They looked at me. In the fast and sudden silence, they came in closer, not talking, but each one of them was slowly and very methodically removing their ulsters, mackintoshes and umbrellas. Their eyes were undressing me. I could see that. Desperate smiles tugged at their lips. Their expressions were frightening. Every single one of them had only one thing in mind. They couldn't take their eyes off my crotch. I had to restrain a crazy desire to make like September Morn. I felt as naked and defenseless as that famous calendar girl.

"Now, ladies—" I began. "This is all very simple, really—"

No one spoke. They kept on coming, as if by some silent mutual contract. I began to wonder who would get the drumsticks and who would get the wishbone. They were all very young, no more than eighteen by the looks of their clean, unmarked faces. All blondes, of course. It was my time of life for blondes and virgins. I also had a feeling none of them spoke English. Who at a Skoda Works would, really? Especially if these were all young dolls from the peasant class.

Peasants, hah. High-born women didn't have what these broads did. As the disrobing continued, all I could see were huge, melon-round teats and superbly rounded hips. The women were beginning to titter now, a bit nervously, as if the time had come to draw straws for the man who had been ingested with the magical silver pills.

They began to talk now. A babble of Russian and Czech and I picked out a word here and there—like *"cute!"* and *"enormous!"* and the Russky equivalent of *"hot damn!"*—but I was lost until Katie showed up. Where the hell was she, the little heartbreaker? Doing her fingernails?

Now the women were completely naked and flexing their muscles. One of them turned to lock the door. That wouldn't do—Katie wouldn't be able to get in to save me. I panicked.

I retreated and the women closed in. Slowly, taking their time. Their areolas blinked at me like eight more pairs of eyes. Their fuzzy Venus mounds mocked me. They stuck their tongues out. They began to laugh. They were happy. Hell, with the silver pill, I'd be able to service them all—according to what they had heard and hoped was true. I was in one helluva spot. I could handle eight broads, but on my terms and speaking English. This way they could ruin me. I began to sweat. My mouth was drier than Texas.

They were sweating too. But in a different way. The oils and tensions of passions made all of their carnal bodies sleek and dewy and—downright scary. They were looking at me like a bunch of animals now.

"K-K-K-KATIE!" I yelled.

The women stopped, looked at each other questioningly, then all shrugged like a vaudeville act and kept on coming. They all smiled as if to placate a nervous tiger. I was trapped. I'd have to screw my way out or die. And be food for the worms.

The first woman to reach me, a peaches-and-strawberry blonde, extended her arm and touched my crotch. She blurted something with hoarse enthusiasm. The rest of her pals whooped happily and closed in for the kill. One of them was so beside herself, she was holding herself open with both hands. I closed my eyes. I couldn't look. Mammaries loomed.

And then Katie's sweet, bright voice broke up the party. Only temporarily. I heard a rapid-fire machine-gun string of words that must have been Czechoslovakian, and then nobody moved. Then more words and I could feel the women drawing back. I opened my eyes. I was saved by the belle of Betchnika.

At what price?

She was standing in the center of the naked females, her expressive hands and eyes going full blast. I looked around the place, wondering how she had gotten in with the door locked. I saw a small window without frame or glass beyond the next pillar that supported the roof of the building. I watched Katrina Walsky. Whatever she

106

was telling the women seemed to go down the right way. They were all nodding happily, flinging me loving looks and then listening to Miss Walsky again. I frowned. I couldn't make heads-or-tails of it.

Finally the women all chorused their approval and Katie came over to me. I could see the women scooping a handful of straw off the floor and starting to draw lots. I frowned. They were like a bunch of excited schoolgirls playing spin-the-bottle.

"You took your time getting here," I growled. "What kept you?"

"I watched from the window. You were beautiful in your fear. So tall, so proud, so unafraid."

"Hooey. What did you tell them that's got them so agreeable?"

She laughed but the laugh was bittersweet. A pulse was jumping in her smooth neck and her whim-whams were shaking. She was mad too.

"It was easy. I promised them each a half hour with the new Russian Tarzan. This was your idea, remember? In exchange for that, I'll be able to ask them about the other men they've waylaid, how long they lasted and all that. Okay? I know you can do it, but I'm plenty jealous. It won't be fun standing around watching you do some other girl. Girls."

"Yeah—" I muttered. "But eight—"

"S'matter, Damon? Lost your touch?" She was being deliberately bitchy, but she was a woman in love and it was natural female reaction. Still, I had my work cut out for me. I'd had such a good time with Katie I wasn't that horny anymore. You know how you feel about food after you've had a full meal.

"A half-hour," I grumbled. "Couldn't you have made it ten minutes each? That's all it will take to make them well-done."

"That's up to you. I don't care how you do it, but do it, and then I'll question each one as you finish. Rod—"

"Yeah?"

"Think you can save enough for me? Standing around watching is going to make my blood pressure go way up. After all, this is still so new to me."

I winked at her and patted her head. I began to undress. With great slowness, measuring my opponents. A dozen sexual plans were racing through my mind. Eight women was going to be a chore, no matter how much fun. I might have to invent a few things. Even old Arabs are happy with no more than about six sirens.

"Don't worry," I said. "For you, there'll always be a Rod Damon. I'll damn well save the best part for you."

"You'd better," she warned. "I'm still the commissar's daughter. I could turn you in and win the Lenin Medal."

"Ouch. Stop clowning. Not even in jest."

She laughed, still with tears in it.

"All right. I won't. Do what you have to do and be damned. I'll stick to my part of the bargain." She turned her back and walked away and I saw the peaches-and-strawberries blonde walking toward me with a sappy smile of victory on her face. And her hips undulating and her breasts pushing out to be had. She was holding up a short straw. A very short straw. She'd obviously won the honor of getting Firsts.

Damon Firsts.

And the rest would be getting Sloppy Seconds.

And Thirds.

And Fourths.

And Fifths.

And Sixths.

And Sevenths.

And Eighths!

I almost lost my nerve.

Now that I gave it some serious thought, having enough to satisfy this cock-hungry crowd was going to take everything I had. And more. And worse than that, I couldn't be *that* sure I would have any desire or stamina left to accommodate Katrina Walsky.

That would be a terrible blow to my pride.

And it would hurt Katie awfully, maybe flip her Id, and scar her Psyche forever. I had to make good. For my sake, for the sake of the investigation, for the full glory of the Thaddeus X. Coxeman Foundation. After all, like Walrus-moustache was always fond of saying, wasn't I the Greatest Coxeman of Them All?

Grimly, I got naked.

The strawberry-peaches beauty waltzed into my arms.

The rest of the women, and Katie, watched. My trial by ordeal was going to have a lot of witnesses.

What if I were found wanting?

No, no—a thousand times No!

I'd rather be dead than say *"Uncle!"*

CHAPTER ELEVEN

Eight hungry foreign-language broads.

Well, there was a universal language—sex—and in that department, I have all the degrees and diplomas known to mankind. And womankind.

So I knew what I had to do.

My first victim, peaches-and-strawberries, didn't have a chance. I grabbed her, threw her down on the nearest stack of old hay and before she could open her mouth to breathe, I dicked her and decked her good. With a few incredibly short, savage strokes, each one well calculated to explode all she had in her and leave her spent and limp, needing to recuperate, I rolled off her and hollered, "Next!" That dame must have come three times before she came up for air. She was glassy-eyed and dazed, lying to one side.

The next longest straw, a vulgar-looking, sensuous, hippy young kid came rushing at me. I caught her without getting off the floor, and trapped her nicely before she could crush me. As soon as the glory pole snagged her pit, she let out a shriek and tried to keep from getting killed. As soon as I reversed our positions, and laid her on her back, shafting vigorously, she too had to crawl off to one side to sympathize with the peaches-and-strawberries blonde. "Next!" I shouted again and the third of the hungry octette joined the game. This one was wiser than the others. She didn't attack me. She lay down next to me and waited for me to come to her. I did. I stood on my hands and leaped over, coming down for a one-point landing. Her scream of pleasure must have made the blood of the others run cold. Hell, I didn't need a half-hour with each of these numbers. None of them seemed to have had a good screwing in months. So everything they had to give, gushed forth in rapidfire sequence. Me,

I was just warming up. From one corner of my eye, I could see Katie, trying not to look, busying herself by asking the first two a lot of questions in a stage whisper. I didn't pay any attention. Number Three was pawing the ground weakly, begging me to stop before I killed her and Number Four was charging me. Raring to screw and out to show her lesser buddies how—she *thought*.

This one I grabbed by the ankles, turned her upside down and began walking around the room in the *Standing And Jumping* ploy which ancient Egypt had made an integral part of their fertility rites. Poor Number Four—she got the best tattooing so far, but I nearly killed her. As was usual with the family jewels—once my attitude was whetted, my tool was sharpened into a blunt instrument of incredible strength and longevity. Or should I say —*length?*

Either way, Number Four crawled away from me on all fours, her rear end pulsating and Number Five approached me cautiously, hungry as she was. The storehouse was filling with the moans and whimpers of the ravaged women who had preceded her. Sounds of sheer sexuality!

I was in my element now, swinging high and cutting in all directions. The creamy hips, the inviting glory pits, the hanging gardens, none of them could overwhelm my drive. And my ambition. I had to finish them off and save myself for Katie. Otherwise, I was in for trouble. I didn't want a commissar's daughter sore at me.

Purposely, remorselessly, and I must admit jubilantly, one by one I slashed my way to the victory. Let them say and let them think it was the mysterious silver pill at work. Hooey. It was all Damon. At least, Katie knew the truth.

I polished off Number Five with a combination of Yankowski's forty-five degrees and Nakoma's one-hundred-dred-and-thirtieth position. The wily old Jap swinger had fashioned a ploy where the woman is walked around the room, back-scuttled all the way. He called it *The Back Door To Lotus Land*. Whatever it was, it made Number Five so ecstatic, she literally fainted on my last shove into her hills of home.

Number Six was the easiest of the lot. A big, busty

110

wench with a very tight slit. It hurt her so much she had to give up, crying in frustration but she calmed down when I let her nibble some of the lettuce leaves surrounding my glorious instrument of desire.

For Number Seven, I combined a little of Spain with a dash of Italy. The old bullfighting charge with some of Saganelli's insensate head-on charge. I backed Number Seven up against the far wall of the storehouse and she went down, with her mouth open, breathing like a steam engine, all passion spent. Her eyes had stars in them.

Number Eight got my best effort. I gave her fifteen minutes of my attention. We curled together in a pinwheel that started at one end of the place and wound up at the other. For each roll of our bodies, I struck once like greased lightning. I think Number Eight got off the most orgasms of all her friends. She must have. She was drooling like the village idiot when we finished. And all the while I could hear Katie making with the questions and answers.

Finally I leaped erect. The swinging senation stayed with me. Eight pairs of unbelieving eyes followed me from various positions of the compass as I marched over to Katie. I was a monument of man.

Katie was flushed, almost embarrassed but I could tell she must have gotten a fund of information and had stolen peeks at all the fun and games. Her clothes were damp with desire. And not from the rain. A dozen beads of perspiration dotted her forehead. She trembled as she saw the look in my eyes.

"Get those clothes off," I snapped. "I'm ready."

"Here—?" she stammered. "In front of all these women? I just couldnt'!" Her eyes looked for the nearest way out.

"Oh, yes, you can. I want to show them how it's really done. I was just warming up."

"Aren't you afraid you'll excite them all over again?" She tried to retreat. I blocked her way and pulled her trenchcoat away from her ripe body. She wore a skirt and sweater again. "Besides—don't you want to hear all the information I , got? It's priceless—just what you wanted—"

"Later. Right now all I'm interested in is my rock and

111

roll girl singer. You want me to rip those duds off you? Get moving!"

In a trance, she obeyed.

Soon she was naked before me. The eight women in the barn *oohed* and *aahed* like so many Lesbians at a dike party. But it wasn't for her shapely goodies, as lovely as that was. It was for me and the glory that is Damon. If anything I had waxed larger and stronger. The women whispered in awe, ringing the room like excited kids who have gone from spin-the-bottle to hump-the-boyfriend.

Katie was tremulous.

"Gee—I don't know what to do—with all these women looking at us—"

"I'll show you." I suddenly dropped to my knees in front of her, trapped her thighs with my hands, and gently began to lave upward. She jerked as if my lips were branding irons and then her body responded. Boy, did it. She closed her eyes, seized my ears and tried to mash my head into her darkest interior. Ah, but I fooled her. I jumped erect and came out of a Limbo-like squat, lifting her all the way off the floor on the end of the Damon instrument. A dame down Calypso way had showed me that one. *The Limbo Of Love.* Katie couldn't help herself. She flipped her lid. Quickly, she lost whatever marbles she had left.

In no time at all, she was threshing, thrashing, reaping wheat and singing the damnedest beat song you ever heard. I let her. If she ever cut that record, she would have revolutionized the music industry. So I whipped right back, a left, front, right and rear savagery of niceness that pretty soon wound up in the damnedest duet right on the floor. Our eight viewers were mesmerized. Who could blame them? Katie was getting her kicks with something extra. I knew Katie. I liked Katie. That made a lot of difference.

Inevitably, Katie was pulling my hair, begging me to stop. She couldn't take anymore. She was sore, wouldn't be able to sit down for a week, to hear her tell it. After all, I'd been pounding her with few interruptions since late yesterday afternoon.

A little tired myself, I stopped, letting her slump to the floor. I stood back and turned to face my audience.

112

The eight women spontaneously burst into applause, blistering their palms with enthusiasm. They couldn't help themselves. After all, they had seen a virtuoso at work—Rod Damon, First Penis of Betchnika. Maybe, the world.

I surrendered to the beauty of the moment.

I bowed.

But Katie was on her feet, tugging at my rump and whispering in my ear. "Come on, Maestro. Let's get out of here before they eat you alive for an encore. I'll promise them you'll come back tomorrow. Okay? As great as you are, I don't think even you can give a repeat performance. What do you say?"

"Good girl," I whispered back. "Get me out of here!"

She did.

Just for the record, and as I suspected, none of the eight factory workers from the Skoda Works, Cannon Section, were virgins.

Back at the Betchnika fleabag of a hotel, we changed out of our wet clothes, took showers without horsing around, and then both lay down on the big bed. The bad thunderstorm was still going full blast, kicking hell out of the windows. It sounded like the end of the world. I didn't care at all, because, man, I was tired. Wouldn't you be?

Katie, who had been strangely silent in the Renault on the way back, now opened up. But at least she didn't sound mad anymore. And how could she be? She'd gotten the greatest going over of her still-young life.

"Rod, you are something. Don't you ever run dry? Even Elsie the Cow——"

"Never mind that. Report!"

She chuckled in the darkness. We lay there, lights out, watching the raindrops pelt the corny, old-fashioned windows of the hotel.

"All right, Chief. It's like this." She took a deep breath. She smelled nice and fresh from the shower. But I *was* tired. I didn't lay a finger on her. "I talked to all the women. Some of them were Russian, most of them Czech. But their stories were all the same. It seems they've had a lot of luck hanging around the Firnl Lab, though there's been a dry spell lately because the scientists are trying

113

all kinds of crazy new tests to hit the right formula on the pills. That's the only answer."

"Gekko and Orkoff?"

"Yes. The women's stories all add up to the same thing. Men's testes are being tested with these silver pills. Gekko and Orkoff are obviously not satisfied because the pill isn't perfect yet. Like with the old men—all it did was run them into the ground. So Gekko and Orkoff have been taking blood pressures, trying exhaustion factors, staying power and length of effectiveness. Junk like that there. They get plenty of willing men, but the results aren't always good. One man went wild with a cow, for instance, and another couldn't get enough no matter how many women he had. He died of a heart attack. You dig?"

"I heard about the man with the cow. Go on."

"Well—" she shrugged. "That's it. There *is* a silver pill. Gekko and Orkoff have it; they're trying every stage of it they can. And meanwhile, back in Betchnika, everybody plays dumb. Thanks to the shadow of Russia. So I don't know where we are with this mystery. Do you?"

"Yes. I'm beginning to see the light." I was too. Walrus-moustache's dire warnings—his eagerness to send me on the mission in the first place—all made sense now. Of a sort. No wonder the silver pill was a threat to the global balance of things. What a secret weapon if it was used for nefarious purposes! "Do you see it too?"

She snorted in the darkness. "What do you mean, Lover?"

"Baby, it's like this. Let's say they make the silver pill one hundred percent foolproof. You know—it will make a man go on for hours without end, without harming him physically. Okay? See what can happen? A group of say one hundred men, armed and fortified with silver pills, could turn Betchnika upside down, because it would ruin the country for the men who didn't have silver pills, their women would revolt and take off with the silver pill supermen and—geezis. Can't you follow that line of thought? Ten thousand men in a larger country, with the same pills, could turn it into a Stud's Heaven. Women would leave their families for some action like that. Psychologically the men left behind, their husbands, would be emasculated and probably commit suicide, *en masse.* Total masculine self-destruction of the cuckolds. And then those countries would be ripe for takeover. At a pleasurable price. What a sceme. What a spot for satraps! No wonder the Reds are interested in this pill. It's better than bullets or atom bombs. Not nearly as messy, either."

Katie shivered.

"It sounds—terrible. And if you are right, what can we—you—do about it? You're only one man. Even if you are kinda special and superhuman."

"Right now, I'm just thinking out loud. Let's consider the possibilities." I counted in the dark. *"One*—kill the scientists. Not too good—they might have follow-up boys to ring in and take over where Gekko and Orkoff left off. *Two*—find a neutralizer. No good. How can we neutralize what isn't even perfected yet? *Three*—make our own silver pill. Again risky, and we don't know how far behind we are right now. *Four*—spoil the pills so that Moscow loses all interest in any further research. Now, that one—that one is a definite possibility."

She laughed harshly.

"That's silly. How could you spoil the pill? You don't even know what it's made up of."

"No, but *you* could, my little pet. You majored in biology at Prague University, I hear tell. And you'd do anything for me, wouldn't you?"

"Like what?"

"Like helping me scrap the silver pill project."

"Oh."

"Scared?"

"Yes, definitely. Do you realize we'd have to sneak into the Firnl Lab? That there are probably armed guards? And Gekko and Orkoff know me. They know my father—"

"That could make it easier—what do you say, Katie? It's for me, for Uncle Sam, and it could get you to Hollywood when all the shouting's over."

"I'll do it. When do you want to start?"

"Like tomorrow, Katie. Before they perfect the pill and get going in earnest. But we'll have to make some plans."

She rolled over on her side, facing me. I saw her eyes

gleaming in the dark. The rain was still beating the hotel windows.

"Okay. Tomorrow. Good night, Lover. I'm beat."

"Me too."

About two minutes went by. She stirred uneasily and before I knew it her hand had slid over my stomach and rested directly above the heart of the matter. Her fingertips were curiously restless.

"Rod, baby?" She sounded like a little girl.

"Mmmmmm."

"I'm shameless."

"Why?"

"I'm oversexed. I want—it—again. Can you imagine? After all we did since last night. I got the damnedest itch and burning sensation in the pit of my stomach—"

"Uh huh."

She spoke again. "You really couldn't—get it up again —or could you?" There was hopelessness in her voice.

"Well—"

"I mean if you can't, I understand—gee willies, after all you did today. I mean, how can any man— *RODDDDDDDDDD!*"

There are indeed times when action speaks louder than words.

After all, when it came to sex, as far as Katrina Walsky was concerned, I was the guy that invented the thing.

What else did she have to go by? Who else?

Gee, willies!

So the rain continued to come down and ten thousand busy little fingers and sensations beat rhythmically in Katie's body, heart and soul. She began to hum again, in her own private way, as she always did now when she was happy.

Funny thing.

For the very first time, I noticed that she *did* have a pretty fair voice. I'm no musical expert, but she sounded nice and jumpy and tuneful. She had the beat. That's all you really need.

"Oh, Rod—" She was bubbling with responses, love and admiration. I was plucking her like a banjo, getting a nice pitch on every single one of her strings.

"Yes, my pet?"

116

"Your dong was made for loving—"

"So what else is new?"

She laughed deep in her breasts and piloted her mouth down to my waterline. She fanned her warm, fresh breath over me.

"Nothing," she said. "But lie still now. And stop moving around for a minute, will you? I want to give you something nice and restful. Something you won't have to work so hard for. Okay? Now be a good boy and lie still—this is a present from me to you."

It was.

Hot Lips Walsky had an ace up her own sleeve.

Now I knew what she had done all those restless years of being squired by Betchnika beaus and teenagers. She had perfected her own art until she had waited for the right man to come along. I closed my eyes and throbbed happily as she soloed on the licorice stick.

Gee willies—she was great at it!

CHAPTER TWELVE

Early the next morning, while Katrina Walsky checked back into the family roost again, to allay Poppa Commissar's suspicions once more, I raised Walrus-moustache on the phone again, using the secret code phone number I always used on assignments. I had a few questions for the old buzzard, as well as the data to deliver. He didn't seem too surprised to hear from me again. Betchnika had awakened to another day of sun. The long heavy rain had washed everything fresh and pretty so that the view of the cobbled streets from the telephone booth was downright charming. I hadn't wanted to use the phone in the hotel lobby anymore. After the business with Christina Ketch-Chris, I didn't trust the sleepy old clerk anymore either.

A couple of wide-hipped Betchnika maids, pretty as pictures in their peasant dresses, walked by the booth, giggling and giving me the onceover. I stuck out my tongue at them and turned my back. They looked insulted, tilted their big asses into the air and walked on.

It was my nickel so I got right down to cases, pouring

117

out all the scoop that Katie had given me and adding yesterday's adventurous experiment with the women I had picked up hanging around the Firnl Laboratory. It was quite a report and Walrus-moustache was keenly appreciative of my services. He complimented me roundly. Something he seldom does.

"Brilliant, Damon. Brilliant! You see now what this silver pill means in terms of the world balance of peace?"

"Yeah, I see. I also see what a double-dealing bastard you are."

"I beg your pardon?" His voice retreated into stiff formality. He always does that too when you catch him in a lie.

"Beg, schmeg. Don't tell me you didn't know that Christina Ketch was a double-agent. A fag as beautiful as a woman and as strong as John Wayne. When are you going to give me a break and really level with me when you send me on these assignments? You're going to get my balls chopped off one of these days if you keep it up!"

His sigh exploded the Transatlantic Cable.

"Damon, forgive me. We suspected. We couldn't be sure. What better way than to send you to join him—her in the net? We were sure you would learn the truth. And you did?"

"Yes. And almost got me killed. But I got lucky. The emergency contact is a genius girl. We gave Chris the same medicine she dished out to the twenty-five old men."

"Splendid. But be careful. With their man in the field out of the way, the enemy will be suspicious—"

"I'm not so sure. Moscow is playing this one pretty close to the vest. They don't want to draw more attention to the Firnl Lab than they have to. Seems this is all highly experimental. Do the names Gekko and Orkoff mean anything to you?"

"Yes. Two of the top chemists to come out of the Kremlin. I knew this was important. What about them?"

Briefly I explained about Katie's house, Katie's Poppa and the many evening chats at home with Gekko and Orkoff. Walrus-moustache, listening patiently, did not interrupt save for a cluck or two.

"God, it's bigger than I thought. Damon, what's your next move?"

"I'm going to scuttle the pill, if I can. Doctor it up, make it tricky and unreliable and make Moscow drop its plans for it here in Betchnika."

"And how pray will you do that? These men are no fools—" He was skeptical, as he had every right to be. All ramrods and bosses are.

"Let me try. I'll call you back if I have to holler for help."

"Very well. I trust your judgment—when you aren't naked and making love. At times like now, you sound coherent, very intelligent and on the job. I like you better that way, you know."

"I love you too. One thing I can't figure out though."

"What's that?"

"If Chris was a phony and had killed all those old men, why come back to town with me, asking a lot of questions he already had the sneaky answers to?" That was still bothering me a lot.

"Damon, Damon." He was tolerantly amused.

"I said something stupid?"

"Afraid so, my boy. Don't you see? They learned outside countries were investigating. This Chris went along with you, simply in order to see how much we knew and at the same time, uncover any other contacts we might have had planted in Betchnika. Lucky for us, and for you, you beat him to the punch."

He was right. It was stupid of me not to have guessed that. I'm telling you—this James Bond business isn't as simple as it looks. It's twisted, crazy, double-dealing and plenty dangerous.

"Lucky for me," I agreed. "Well, gotta run. I'll call back as soon as I make some progress. And, dear Walrus-moustache, see what you can do about arranging a Hollywood screen test for Katrina Walsky. We owe her a lot. Call Zanuck, if you have to. She really has a very fine singing voice and she looks a helluva lot better than Streisand does."

"Really? Well, I'll see what I can do. I don't know Zanuck, but Joe Levine is a friend of mine. Well, we'll see. Damon. Do take care of yourself. The Foundation wouldn't be the same without you."

"Sure. Who else can you push around?"

119

"Now, that's not fair. I'm very fond of you and you know it—"

"Of course you are. Maybe you're queer for me?"

"Goodbye, Damon," he said icily from all those miles away. "Try to drop dead." He hung up, leaving me laughing to myself.

I went back to my hotel room and waited for Katie to come in or call back. My mind was flying. My plans, hastily thought out the night before, needed some refinements. But I was convinced somehow that before I could do anything about the Firnl Lab, where the pills were sure to be, I had to get the drop on Gekko and Orkoff somehow. I wanted very badly to listen in the very next time they dropped in on Poppa Walsky for a glass of beer. A little knowledge, the right kind, in advance, can go a very long way.

While I waited, I did some Yoga exercises, ran around the room a few times and then took a shower. The room was breezy with the fine, balmy weather, so I sat around in the buff and did some homework, using the old Betchnika Hotel stationery in the small secretary in the corner. I had not idea how long Katie would be. Maybe Poppa was scolding her for staying out so late again. Anyhow, I found a pencil and wrote up some notes and things on the thesis I was preparing for the fall semester at the university. I was doing a paper on *The Older Woman And Her Sexual Superiority As A Lover*. The libraries of the world had countless tomes on that subject, but I was hitting it from the purely explicit tact of the bedroom. For openers, as I sat and thought, I scribbled down some of the more easily memorable comments of the world's great lovers on the subject. It would make a very cunning and attractive foreword.

There was, of course, the old standby from Europe:

"You have to get some fun out of life even if it's with a grandmother in bed."

—An old German proverb.

And of course—

"In women, the aging process starts from the neck down."

—Benjamin Franklin, in a letter

120

I always liked this one too:

"Give me mothers, widows, divorcees and seasoned women. Keep your ingenues and sweet young things for yourself. I much prefer the ripe cherry to the green olive."

—Marcel Alevoinne, 1873-1924

England didn't do so badly, either:

"I love the fall and winter. The spring and the summer are like frivolous maids who cannot make up their minds. Ah, but that stretch of time twixt October and March, there for all the world to see is Mother Nature with her mind truly made up, her intentions all too clear, her meaning inviolate. She takes off her clothes in public, as it were—

—Lord Ashton in his *Memoirs des Amour*

Those would be great words of advice for openers. Even on the printed page, they glowed with truth. No kidding. Who do you think would be the better lay—an eighteen-year-old rookie or a seasoned veteran in her thirties or more? Hell, yeah. Natalie Wood's a knockout, but I'll bet she couldn't match a Magnani in the hay.

Apart from gratitude, the Over-Forty Club are sensational sexual partners. Like the old saying goes: they won't tell, they won't swell, and they're as grateful as hell!

Anyway it promised to be a very stimulating paper, because my research of a few months earlier had included some fieldwork with a countess, a snake charmer, an actress, a dancer, a housewife and a white-collar worker, all of whom had seen younger days. Each of them had been almost insatiable and doubly rejuvenated by Sex. If I hadn't been Damon, I don't think I could have made any of them say *"Uncle!"* Older women just don't know when to stop. The sky's the limit, in a word. They hump like there's no tomorrow for them.

I was well into my notes and data when Katie came trooping in breathlessly again from the street. Her eyes were shining, as they always were when she saw me, and her fine abundant figure was sweatered bumpily and skirted humpily, as ever.

We kissed warmly and I waited for her to catch her breath.

"Poppa spank?"

"Not at all. He was glad to get me out of the house again and didn't even know I was missing. Besides, it seems that Gekko and Orkoff are coming to dinner again."

It was perfect. Like a hole-in-one. And I don't mean golf.

"Great. That ties in nicely with our first step in the new plan." I rubbed my hands together briskly.

She groaned aloud. "Now what are you up to?"

"I want to eavesdrop tonight while your Poppa pow-wows with those guys. It's the only way. We may learn something more about the pills. We can't go barging into that lab, looking high and low. Remember, I'm counting on you to mix up the formulas and louse up the deal for them. Otherwise, we've accomplished nothing."

"Isn't there a safer way? Our house is pretty small. I don't see how I can sneak you in—no, it's too risky."

"Don't argue. It's got to be." Another light went on in my brain. "Hell, what's to worry? Bring me home with you before dinner. As a new beau. Then I'll pretend to leave and double back. Your house have a garden? Trees? Plenty of shrubs? It'll be easy. I'm an old Eagle Scout from way back."

"Well—" She was still troubled.

"Katie, you want to go to Hollywood? I called my friend this morning. He's going to talk to Zanuck and Joseph Levine."

"My house," she said, "is a ranch-type place. Surrounded by a wall of ivy. There's a lot of trees and a French door leading into the garden, and you wouldn't have any trouble at all. Honest."

"That's my old Katie," I laughed. "Want to make love before we start out on our enterprise? It still is a bit too early to take a beau home to see your house."

"Do you have to ask?"

"No, but it's considered polite where I come from."

"Then my answer is Yes, and my God, how do you keep on going like that? Don't you ever wear out?"

"It's a short life and a merry one," I said. "Get out of those duds and get on the bed."

Katie performed both activities with remarkable speed, and since I was already naked, I merely joined her on the percales. The sun warmed our bodies and we began our love games. Slowly, gently and with great tenderness, until the savage beast claimed us both and we became a whirlwind of rotating rumps and churning thighs. I laid her good.

I forgot about the work on my thesis.

Older dolls are all I said they were, but there's nothing wrong with a seasoned virgin either.

Katie had learned quickly and well.

I was hard put to keep up with her.

But I did.

So she laid me but I laid her.

We went spinning and sinning into our own private world of pune, tune and half-moon. She could have set it to music all right.

We had a ball in Betchnika, Damon style.

That's the only way to travel in bedrooms.

Ask the girl that owns one.

Poppa Commissar's house was all that Katie had indicated. When we reached it at sundown in the Renault, Katie parked the car in a plain, bare garage just behind the house. The building was a ranch, indeed, and thoroughly in keeping with the Communist platform of the bare necessities. No frills, no ornaments, just brick and stone and plain common clay. The trees and the shrubbery and the ivy-colored walls closed out the rest of the Betchnika world. There was no other car in the garage.

"What a break," Katie enthused. "Poppa's out and nobody's home. All I have to do is stash you in my bedroom. It's a cinch."

"No servants or maids?" It was too good to be true.

"Uh-uh. On Poppa's salary? Tsk, tsk. Besides, he has to show Moscow how frugally he can live on their salary. I'm still wearing my high school prom formal. I was big for my age."

123

"You still are. Especially around the curves. Okay, let's hurry. How about that bedroom?"

The house was even more spare. Barely furnished. Solid wooden chairs and tables, plain bookcases without glass, no fancy rugs or jars or bric-a-brac. Katie's room was at the far end of the building. It was slightly warmer-looking. A big bed, a bigger closet area, but at least she had dollied it up a bit. With nice curtains, some fresh flowers in a vase and the walls were a mosaic of show business luminaries, especially vocalists, male and female. Glossies of Tom Jones outnumbered the Frank Sinatras by about five to two. Katie led me to the bed, sat me down and clasped my hands. Her eyes searched my face.

"You be careful now, you hear? I don't want anything to happen to you."

"Nothing will. When Poppa and Gekko and Orkoff show up, you go on about your business and I'll make with the ears. We're bound to learn something. Besides, you've already told me what you could do with the pills if you ever get your hands on them."

She nodded. "Wouldn't be hard. I told you—I know they contain some strychnine as an aphrodisiac. So it would be ABC biological snaps to alter the strychnine solution—not quite enough to kill but enough to change the formula and effect drastically. We could substitute saltpetre in the other pills and really goof things up that way too. Boy, would that confuse Gekko and Orkoff! Imagine giving a man a silver pill, expecting orgiastic miracles, and getting a cat too bored to get an erection! That I gotta see."

"You will. You've been swell, Katie, and if you don't get that Hollywood offer, I quit."

"Don't do that. At least you tried," she said, almost shyly.

A car horn suddenly blared in the stillness outside. Katie's eyes flew open. We could hear tires slithering on the driveway.

"Poppa! Quick get under the bed. He probably went down to pick Gekko and Orkoff up the way he always does when the lab closes for the day. Oh, hurry—"

It was the age-old situation. Don't get caught in the female's bedroom when Poppa comes home, even if this

124

time the reasons were a bit different. I squeezed under the bed and was faced with rows of shoes. Sneakers, sandals, loafers, high heels, the works. Maybe Poppa had to scrimp but Katie was nuts about shoes. At least they didn't smell. I burrowed down behind them. I heard Katie go to the door, step through and walk down the hall. Now, gruff voices muffled from the front of the house. Real Russian bears. They always came on like a circus act. I waited, straining to listen. I heard Katie greet her father and his friends and offer some trumped-up story about coming back to change her clothes. Somebody grunted something in Czech. It must have been her father and the noises died off. But I heard glasses tinkling. Russians also like to drink. Then footsteps sounded in the hallway, again, and Katie was back in the room. She sat down on the bed in front of me, her nice ankles in view. She was trembling. Spy-nerves, I guessed.

"What's the matter?"

"He wants me out of the house. So he can be alone with them. Oh, Rod, I'll have to leave."

"That's okay," I whispered. "Just as well. They won't expect me to be here. You go. I'll see you later."

She reached down under the bed, offering her lips. I kissed them. Her eyes were worried.

"You be careful. And don't be long. Find out what you have to and get out. I'll wait down the road about three hundred yards with the car. Okay?"

"Deal. Scat, now. The sooner I do this, the better off we'll all be. Thanks, Katie."

"For what?" she rasped. "They find you here, they'll line you up against the town hall wall and shoot you. You know that, don't you?"

"Will you beat it?"

"Oh, *you!*"

Tearfully she leaped off the bed and flounced from the room. Her shoes walked down the hall, quickly and fearfully. I heard her say goodbye to Poppa Walsky and then the front door slammed and the house went all quiet again. The men all laughed.

This was it.

I was alone in the house with the men who had the answer to the silver pill enigma.

Today, Silver Pills.
Tomorrow the World!
Not if I could help it.

I sneaked out from under the bed, slid over to the door, peered out and listened. A low hum of conversation flowed from the other end of the house. Poppa was already in conference with his two Fed jackals. I was in luck. They were speaking English!

The hall was narrow, dim and empty. I eased down it, keeping close to the wall. I had to move in a hurry if something happened. There was no telling what in a strange house you are in for the first time. I hoped to hell there weren't any household pets, like a dog or a cat or a talking parrot. I wanted to kick myself in the ass for not asking Katie about a little item like that. Some spy I am. James Bond could take lessons from me I was so smart.

Suddenly a telephone rang somewhere.

I froze to the wall. My heart flip-flopped.

Heavy shoes, sounding like clodhoppers, thundered on the wooden floor of the house. I didn't dare breathe.

The phone stopped ringing as somebody picked it up and I let my breath out again. For a second I didn't know whether it was the phone in Katie's bedroom or not. I lost about a pound sweating that one out.

Then a man cursed and laughed out loud.

"Wrong number!" a voice boomed. It must have been Poppa Walsky. He sounded darling. A real peach. "Forgive me, gentlemen! More wine, Orkoff? Take another drink, Gekko! We must discuss the pill—"

Bingo.

My shot in the dark had worked. I had come to the right place.

More glasses tinkled.

They sounded like they were settling down to some serious drinking. That was fine with me. Men swacked and plastered are more inclined to be looser with their tongues. Ask any bartender.

I slipped down the short hallway. Drawing closer to the sounds of revelry. All of the men, including Poppa Walsky, had big gruff voices. Real bears all the way. I

126

guess it goes with the Russian weather. Even if Poppa was a Czech.

I stopped where the hall ended and waited.

There was a pause.

And then Gekko or Orkoff said, almost sadly, "There is nothing else we can do. We haven't perfected it as yet. To continue our experiments in Betchnika, we would have to show our superiors a far more improved pill. As it is, I fear we shouldn't try any more experiments here. It may create riots, unrest—what with the Russo-Czechoslovakian situation as it is, I think it wiser if myself and Orkoff moved on."

"No," Poppa Walsky pooh-poohed the idea. "Try a little longer, eh? You can never tell."

"Yes," the third man, Orkoff, chimed in. "Walsky is right, Gekko. We can try a few more tests. We have the willing men and the women this time. But nothing like that foolhardy risk we took with the old men. That was a mistake. The old fools!"

"Moscow could have had our heads for that," Gekko agreed. "Very well—one more major experiment. Silver Pill Number Seventy-Nine. I hope we manage something this time."

They drank to that. Glasses clinked.

"Besides," Gekko continued, his voice blurred with wine. "What if some fool commissar comes down from Moscow to check our progress? He could have us booted out of the project because of our failures. You know how those swine like to curry favor with the Party."

"*Da, da,*" Orkoff muttered feelingly. "And then take all the credit too. If any. Very well. We try once more. I'm sure we can come up with something this time. Day after tomorrow, I will give our men Number Seventy-Nine. See what happens—"

More talk flowed and I turned around and went back down the hall. I slipped back into Katie's room and went to the window. I had heard enough. More than enough. Gekko himself had provided the solution. I knew what I had to do. I opened Katie's window and dropped out into the garden. It was no trouble at all to stalk through the garden, leaving by a side gate and go down the road to where Katie was waiting for me. The sun was well down behind the trees when I spotted the Renault. My mind was tingling with expectation.

Gekko had opened his big mouth and now I knew how to scuttle the project known as Silver Pill.

I wondered if my Russian was good enough to pass muster in the Firnl Laboratory.

If I could get my hands on a proper uniform, Commissar Damonski was going to pay a required call on Gekko and Orkoff at the Firnl Lab. At the special request of the Kremlin.

After all, what progress did they have to report to Moscow after all these months of research, money and futility!

CHAPTER THIRTEEN

The next twenty-four hours were a whirlwind of activity. My next and greatest plan was about to be fulfilled. But believe me, I couldn't have done a thing without Katrina Walsky. On Operation Silver Pill in Betchnika she was absolutely indispensable. When I told her about my plan in the Renault going back to town, she kept shaking her head, saying it wouldn't work; but in the end, she finally capitulated. And I didn't have to threaten her with Hollywood, either. She had become my woman and I was her man. Variations *Lover, Baby* and *Rod*. When she was really hung on me, she called me something that sounded like *putchinksa* which must be the Czech version of *Pussycat* or *Tiger*.

Anyway, she worked her rump off for me for the better part of that day. The sun was gone but we needed the dark to operate in. Boy, did we ever.

First she got her hands on a commissar's uniform for me. It was about a size too small but that didn't matter. All it did was emphasize my height and size, and since I wanted to impress Gekko and Orkoff the next day, that was all to the good. It seemed the local Little Theatre in Betchnika to which Katie belonged (she kept telling me how she had knocked them in the aisles playing *Hedda Gabler*) put on a lot of plays with Russian Communist plots and scenes. So there were plenty of Red uniforms in the Property House behind the theater, which was more like a barn than anything I've ever seen. It figured. Who would expect the Reds to subsidize a little theater and lay out some rubles for overhead?

Secondly, under cover of night, I drove her out to the Firnl Laboratory and went into my own Jimmy Valentine routine. The place was deserted, having closed hours ago, and there were no lusting women hanging about this time. So we crept onto the property and I jimmied open a rear window and helped her climb in. Luckily, she had visited the lab a few times with Poppa Walsky and she knew the layout. There were no guards, not even a nightwatchman. I tell you we have to beat the Reds, one way or another. They skimp and cut corners in the wrong places. I waited for her outside, keeping the Renault parked in the same place she had the day before. Her biology background was going to be put to the acid test.

"Remember," I warned her before she disappeared into the inky interior of the place, "look for Number Seventy-Nine experiment. That's the one they're going to try next. It's that or nothing."

"Oh, I know, I know," she whispered nervously. "How many times do you have to tell me?" Then she was gone and I went back to the car to sit, smoke and listen to the crickets. She was gone a long time, like an hour, and the moon had come out and I'd gone through half my pack of butts before I saw her cutting across the spooky lawn that surrounded the place, like a shapely ghost. I jumped with fear when she materialized.

When she got back into the car, she was shivering.

"Did you shut the window after you? Remember, this has to be perfect. No slip-ups."

"Yes, damn you. What a job!"

"How did it go?"

She folded her hands. "Like a Swiss watch. The lab has all the facilities. I took the whole load of Number Seventy-Nine—there was about a hundred silver capsules, emptied them and switched the ingredients like we said. I doubled the strychnine in some, added saltpetre to others and used some other chemicals lying around the place. If that silver pill isn't screwy now, it never will be!"

"That's my girl. I'm proud of you."

"You should see those pills. Kind of an inch long, all silver on the outside. Must be a sugar-coated outside, tasting like sugar. A fifty percent solution."

"Skip the technical stuff. Now, we'll drive back to town and I'll brush up on my Russian with you on the way."

"Why? Gekko and Orkoff like to speak English. They show off with it. Being bi-lingual is a mark of culture. You know that."

"Just in case. Now, hear me recite the alphabet, then I'll do numbers and some of the standard comments like *Hello, Goodbye* and *Good Morning*. My accent's pretty good."

She shook her head as I backed the Renault out to the roadway, turned around and headed back to town. She was worried about me again, as she had since I first outlined the plan.

"Forget the language problem. What if Gekko and Orkoff ask for credentials? What if they decide to phone Moscow to confirm your visit? What if they demand to know who you really are—then what? Huh? You'll be a dead duck and I'll cry the rest of my life."

"Don't worry. You don't know the Red mind like I do. I studied in Russia for a year on a grant. If I squawk loud enough, act officious and tough, they'll step in line. And I got an ace in the hole. They won't be able to check me out in Moscow."

She snorted. "Why? You going to drive around town now cutting all telephone wiring?"

"Not necessary, my fine feathered female. You're forgetting what day tomorrow is."

She frowned. "The first of May. So what?"

"So what? It's *May Day!* Russia's biggest holiday. Nothing will be open in Moscow. Nothing official anyway. They wouldn't dare get huffy about it tomorrow. It would be like spitting in Lenin's face!"

"Rod!" she squealed with delight, throwing her arms around my face. I almost hit a rabbit which hopped across the roadway in my car lights. "You're a genius. You really are—and I thought you only had a penis for a brain. Not that I minded—"

I chuckled, feeling good. She was a yummy broad. Great company in or out of bed.

"I," I said, "manage to use my other head once in a while."

She laughed. "Two heads *are* better than one."

"Never mind that. What are you going to do about your father tomorrow? I don't want him at the Firnl because I want you there and your old man might get in the way."

"Don't worry about him. I'll put enough sleeping powder in his oatmeal to make him sleep all day. He's got a lot of allergies anyway and the doctor prescribed a whole load of tranquilizers for him to cut down on the pain and discomfort. Forget about Poppa. I'll take care of him."

She sounded like she still remembered Mamma and what Poppa Walsky had done to her. So I did what she told me. I forgot about Poppa Walsky, the commissar of Betchnika. He would not get in the hair of Commissar Damonski of Moscow.

The next great thing Katie did for me was to get her hands on a car. A big, impressive looking Daimler that looked like it might have come from the big cities. It seemed she did have a boyfriend or two in town and one of them whose father owned a farm and bet on horse races now and then had managed to buy a big car. She managed to borrow it.

It was the last neat touch.

When Gekko and Orkoff saw me drive up in a Daimler in my nice tight uniform with Poppa Walsky's daughter driving, I'd be in like Flynn. We would account for Poppa's absence with the story of his being indisposed—which would be the flat honest truth if Katie doped his oatmeal properly.

So that was it. We were just about all set for the big chance.

We were ready to move in the morning.

In the meantime, the night was young and she was still beautiful and eager to learn a few more strokes of the art and craft of making it in the sack with a man.

But this time she couldn't stay all night.

She'd have to be on the scene at the house in the morning to give Poppa Commissar the full treatment.

Still, we had time to ball most of the night away before

dawn came creeping in over the mountains and down into the trees. So I showed Katie a few more tricks. Most importantly, I taught her Von Tappen's method of holding-of-orgasm. A highly difficult but very important ploy for those who would stave off the moment of fulfillment to lengthen the amount of time in which to enjoy the sex act. It'd be a fine thing if everyone knew the canny old Kraut's Prussian game, but in reality it would drive most women up the wall. Women have to let go, they have to have their lubricity and fourteen little orgasms along the way. It's different for guys. We pop bigger and at wider intervals, give or take the stamina of the man in question. For me, it's different of course because I am Damon. One of a kind. Still, I like to spread the seeds of knowledge wherever I go. Or whenever I can.

Katie was grateful for the information but she really didn't need it. The average guy she tangled with, once he felt her delicious man-trap close over him, would have let go soon enough. As for herself, she was in her prime with plenty of gas and oil to travel a long way. But the information would come in handy later on when she was much older and would have to be more careful with her energies.

"Gee willies," she panted in my arms as I dipped and retreated, inserted and withdrew everytime I felt myself approach the peak, "that's real cruel. What kind of fun is that? You go away just as soon as I'm ready to spring a leak."

"I am merely demonstrating Von Tappen——"

"Screw Von Tappen! Half the fun is feeling you flood my insides with joy juice. Come on, Rod—give. Cut loose. I want a deluge!"

"Don't you want to learn how to hold back?"

"In a word, no. I didn't give anything up for Lent."

"You are shameless. A hussy. A wanton. A pagan. In short, a very very nice piece of ass."

"If you say so——" she murmured impatiently. Dreamily. Her thighs drove mercilessly around me, digging her heels into my flanks. "Now will you come, please? I'm tired of holding out and as soon as you spill over, I can come up a gusher."

"Make me," I teased.

132

"Damn you!" she panted again, smacking her smooth abdomen into my ribs, jockeying for a fresh position. She engulfed me with her womanliness. The Venus Trap slammed shut. I was caught. I couldn't get out now. So I did her a favor. I cut loose on the rise, letting go a torrent. She cried with happiness. She gushed. Within seconds, we were a deliciously soft, velvety, squirming union of warm fluid.

"Von Tappen!" she snorted. "Hah! What was he, a Nazi?"

"Uh-uh. He left Germany in 1933, went to Brooklyn to live, drove a cab to earn a living and then won a seat at Columbia. And he did it all by burning the midnight oil and cracking a lot of books—"

"And a lot of women too, I'll bet. Anyway, I don't like his method. Who wants to be strong when all the fun is in being weak?"

"You got me there, girl."

She squeezed me by the testicles.

"Nobody's got you," she growled. "And nobody ever will. You've found a home in the world. You with that damn joy toy of yours. So you'll roll all the way, screwing everything in sight. But you'll see. I'll go to Hollywood, become rich and beautiful and famous, and maybe you'll give me a second look again. I'm right, aren't I? You'll be pulling out of Betchnika if tomorrow's plan works?"

"Afraid so. I don't work for myself. My people will want me to go back home and make my report."

"Your people? What are they—all women?"

I laughed. "Your people are my people. The Coxe Foundation. Who pick up the tab for my travels. Now, what do you say we get some sleep, and before dawn we'll drive out to your house."

She yawned, stretching happily. Her splendid body uncoiled like a tigress at play and she turned around, planting her derrière squarely in front of me.

"Don't do that," I warned.

"Why not?"

"I'm an ass man. All I have to do is see one like yours and I'm never too tired. I can't resist an urge to fill it up—"

"You're not scaring me," she whispered sleepily. "You

know that, don't you? If that's your hang-up, go to it, man. With my blessings. Bet you can't keep me from falling asleep."

"Don't bet. You'll lose."

"Prove it."

She had that sort of fanny that fills out East and West like a heart-shaped Valentine. North and South was just as magnificent, full, packed and covered with a skin of pure ivory. I couldn't help myself. What a launching pad for a guided missile. I hugged her, kept my legs closed and shot the bolt home. She didn't move right away, but she was right. She would never be a Von Tappen student. She had too much to give. In no time at all she was pushing back and her roll was jellied in no time at all.

When we finally quit, she subsided with a sigh.

"You win. You always do. Gee willies, why do you *always* feel so good?"

"My heart is always in my work," I reminded her. "And this is the liveliest art I know."

"Goodnight, Michelangelo," she whispered happily.

"Goodnight," I said and rolled over and went to sleep. Our rumps kissed all night.

Somewhere in Betchnika, a pair of dogs barked noisily in the cobbled streets.

I wasn't the only one getting his licks that night.

By dawn, we decamped from the hotel. Katie, bright-eyed and bushy-tailed, drove the Daimler. As soon as we left town limits, I changed my clothes in the back seat. The commissar uniform was as tight as the first time. I felt like my buttons were going to pop. But it was the usual Red miserliness. Plain coarse woolen jacket and pants of a military cut with a soft-billed cap to make it official.

The day promised to be warm again, and by the time Katie drove slowly up the road to her house, it was getting muggy. A threat of rain hung in the leaden, hazy skies. It didn't matter. Today was an indoor operation if all went off without a hitch at the Firnl Laboratory. May Day meant that everything would be closed, but it had to be a perfect day for Gekko and Orkoff to be there to brush up on their research and experimentation. I was

134

counting on that, thanks to what I had overheard in the Walsky hallway.

Katie parked under a bower of concealing trees, turned to kiss me and smiled.

"I look funny?" I asked, worried about the uniform, and my appearance.

"You look just fine. I feel like saying *'Tovarich'!'*"

"No kidding?"

"Would I fool you, man of mine? Give us a kiss before I go in and make like a treacherous daughter."

She kissed me moistly.

"This will only take a sec. But I'll hang around awhile to see if the stuff really works, okay? Give me about a half hour."

"Take your time. We can't get to the Firnl too early. Though I'll bet a million bucks to a ruble that Gekko and Orkoff are down there right now, as early as it is, making like mad scientists."

She nodded, hopped out of the car, waved, and disappeared through a high row of privets, to enter the house by the back door. I waited in the Daimler and smoked a cigarette. I forgot about Poppa Walsky and his Katie. My mind was on the Firnl Laboratory. If my plan worked, I'd be out of Betchnika and on the plane to Munich in less time than it takes to deflower a virgin.

Any virgin.

I was sure of a few things, though.

May Day or not, there would be the same hungry women hanging around the Firnl Lab waiting for their super-charged studs. Sex never takes a holiday. Sex Hunger, that is.

Gekko and Orkoff, if I passed for a visiting Commie official from Moscow, would have to do what I told them. If Katie's monkeying with the silver pills worked, they would have to draw up a bad report and abandon the project. Which was all I was interested in. Me and the Thaddeus X. Coxe Foundation. And Walrus-moustache.

I wondered if he had had a chance to talk to Joe Levine yet about Katie. It would be even tougher to leave her without keeping my promises to her.

The sun had poked its way through the hazy clouds when Katie came skipping back through the privets. She had on a big smile that looked very vengeful. She had been gone exactly forty-five minutes, I realized with a start.

"Well?" I asked as she slid in behind the wheel. She was humming one of her rock and roll classics. Which meant she was happy again.

"Sleeping like a baby. He went right into the mush, face first. I left him there. He'll be all right."

"Good. Let's get going before I lose my nerve altogether." I pulled my cap down over my eyes and tried to look mean. She put the Daimler in gear.

"Firnl Laboratory, home of the Silver Pill," she said with bright chirpiness, "Coming up!"

"Take your time. We don't want to get any tickets."

"From who? Our police force consists of one car, two bicycles and about fifty foot patrolmen, all in town. It's clear sailing from here on in."

"All the same, be careful. Don't run out of gas, either."

"Who me?" She laughed and the big car went spinning out to the roadway, lunged down the lane and sped rapidly away from Poppa Walsky's ranch home. I hoped the good commissar didn't drown in the oatmeal. Disobedience to a parent is one thing, but I frown on patricide. Katie was too adorable and delicious to spend her life rotting away in a Communist jail.

The Daimler ploughed smoothly toward the Firnl Laboratory.

The sun seemed to play tag with us along the way, ducking in and out of the leaden clouds. It was lousy weather, really. Muggy and sticky. I hoped the laboratory was air-conditioned.

After all, when a man is going to get laid, shouldn't he have all the comforts of home and not have to worry about sweating like a pig before he starts?

That's only fair and sensible.

There was one thing I hadn't told Katrina Walsky. I, Rod Damon, intended to join the silver pill experiment myself. If only to prove to Gekko and Orkoff the stunning degree of differentiation and lack of standardization in their faulty pill.

Faced with my kind of performance, they'd have to see they were in trouble. On the wrong track, as it were.

But I kept that to myself as Katie kept on humming and kept on heading for the Firnl Laboratory in the woods.

When we pulled up to the place, things were moving as I expected. As early as the hour was, and it couldn't be later than nine, the lab was already doing its overflow female business. The stone doorway was crowded with loitering peasant women. I even detected an upper-middle class woman or two or three. They all had one thing in common. Hungry eyes, restless bodies and tongue-licking expectancy. My hopes soared. Not even May Day had turned them away. Which meant only one thing to me. Business was going on as usual at Firnl—the scientists had to be there, the male guinea pigs had shown up and word had got around to the man-hungry females of Betch-nika. It wasn't surprising that the regular men of town were not hanging around. Walrus-moustache's theory was correct. Even if the pill still wasn't perfect, it seemed to have shamed the average Betchnikian man into apathetic inactivity. They were all probably home sharpening their razors.

As Katie wheeled the Daimler onto the concrete drive-way, I said, "Honk the horn. Good and loud. We're not sneaking up on Gekko and Orkoff, you know."

She did, blasting the sylvan stillness of the trees and early morn with a tattoo of noisy alarm. The women on the patio turned to look at us, shaking their heads, shooting questions at each other. There was a fresh hopeful-ness in their manner. I recognized some of the eight wantons from the storehouse experiment of the first visit. They wouldn't recognize me, though, unless I took my clothes off. Besides then I was dressed like a Balkan boy scout, this time I was a commissar!

Katie slowed the car to a halt. No one had emerged from the lab.

"Again," I said, indicating the horn. "Make out like it's New Year's on Times Square."

With high glee and her natural love of music, she continued to batter the car horn. Pretty soon, we got results. The women were all laughing now, even if they didn't understand the joke, the front doors of the lab swept open and two besmocked, bewhiskered, curly-haired bears

137

stood bewildered on the threshold. It was Gekko and Orkoff all right. Nobody else could look so Russian, so scientific and so befuddled by the appearance of a very-official looking car from out of nowhere. I caught my breath, pulled my tunic down tighter and got out of the car. Katie came out her side and Gekko and Orkoff spotted her, exchanged glances and then came clattering down the stone steps to see what was up. The waiting women hurled taunts and jibes at them as they came. I yawned very theatrically, dusted off some imaginary lint from my coat sleeve and Katie went to greet Gekko and Orkoff, managing to look awed and proud at the same time. I got the impression as she began to talk to them in Russian that she was explaining all about Poppa Commissar's sudden illness and my very urgent arrival at her house.

Gekko and Orkoff came stumbling over with her, looking perplexed. I gambled on using English and won.

"How many men do you have inside to test for the pill?"

"Ten," blurted one of the beards. "But, Commissar, this is most unexpected and a great honor. But Moscow didn't tell us—"

"Moscow has to tell no one anything." I eyed them coldly. "I am Commissar Damonski, plenipotentiary with sealed orders. You will select ten women from this rabble and follow me—" I strode past them toward the entrance. The old trick. Act like you belong; don't give the enemy time to think; and bluff like mad. "Comrade Walsky," I barked over my shoulder. "Follow me. Inside, you will assist with the technical details and terms. I'll want a full report. Moscow has waited long enough!"

"But, but—" One of the beards was pulling respectfully at my sleeve. I whirled and eyed him up and down. He was medium-sized like his partner and mostly beard with great big popping eyes. "Comrade Commissar, we are not prepared. We must have time. You see, we haven't perfected the project yet. Experiment Seventy-Nine—"

"What is your name?" I snapped coldly.

"Gekko," he stammered. "Boris Gekko. And this is Feodor Orkoff. My colleague. Surely—"

"Comrade Gekko," I poured on the coal. "Moscow is tired of this project. They have sent me down for a final

138

report. This test shall get to be your last. You understand? If this failure continues, you can go finish your project in Siberia! Do I make myself clear?"

"Siberia!" He paled and looked at Orkoff, who was just as frightened and just as pop-eyed. "Orkoff—select ten of the ladies. I shall guide Comrade Commissar into the laboratory."

Katie stood at my elbow, hiding a smile as Orkoff sprang down the steps to make his choices among the women who had picked up a word here and there. There was a great clamor and engulfment of poor Orkoff. Gekko sighed, tried to smile, then ushered us into the building. The Firnl was all stone, all white and antiseptic looking like a hospital. I decided to mix brains with kindness.

"How is it you speak English so well, Gekko?" I asked.

He trembled at the implication and then saw I meant it as a compliment.

"I got my doctorate at U.C.L.A.," he babbled. "It was——"

"Good. Capitalism does have its uses. Now, on to the experiments. I must return to Moscow tonight. Whether you fail or succeed is immaterial to me. You understand? You must produce some form of results at once! If we fail here, we can try the project elsewhere. Come, now. Get on with it."

As he led us down a tiled corridor, Katie came abreast of me and squeezed my hand. I squeezed back. Poor Gekko stumbled over himself in his anxiety to please. Behind us, I could hear Orkoff busily and noisily shouting as he made his selections. Footsteps hammered the tiles behind us as the ten lucky women came hurrying in, babbling like kids at the circus, moaning cries of happiness. Orkoff was having his hands full keeping them toned down.

Gekko was still trying to make friends. To be cordial. To lay out a red rug of welcome from the Firnl to Moscow.

"Commissar Walsky has been most helpful. Sorry he is ill. You are fortunate to have Comrade Katrina to guide you about Betchnika——"

"Yes, yes, of course," I barked. "Come, come, Gekko. Get on with it. There is no more time to lose."

139

There wasn't.

I had to make the plan work; get out; accomplish the mission; and discredit the pill all in just a few hours. Or else it was curtains for Commissar Damonski of Moscow.

And Rod Damon of America.

If it had been possible, I would have kept my testicles crossed for good luck.

CHAPTER FOURTEEN

As I had planned and counted on, Gekko and Orkoff fell all over themselves making me welcome. Anxious to impress the visiting fireman from Moscow, they immediately got down to cases and prepared the experimentation room. Katie seemed to know where it was because she led me directly to it. With that troop of hungry females clamoring at our heels.

Beyond the tiled corridor, there was a large, square, high-ceilinged room that resembled a gymnasium more than anything else. There were mats and pillows and towels hung neatly on racks. A great overhead camera-type object focused down from the ceiling on anything that would take place below.

There were ten men already in the room, stripped down to their jockey shorts, standing around listlessly, pawing the floor like restless stallions. When they saw us coming in, with the women in tow, their eyes opened wider, some winked, some smiled and interest generally quickened. You could tell by some of the jockey shorts taking on too many new bumps. I didn't think they had been given the silver pill yet. It looked like the normal, horny amount of wolfly male interest.

Gekko, all business-like, indicated several camp chairs where Katie and I could sit and watch. Then he whispered in Orkoff's ear and his colleague immediately went to the women to pass on some instructions. It was fantastic. I have never seen ten women undress so fast in my life. There was a whirlwind of skirts, panties, blouses and shoes and stockings and in no time at all, the ten willing women were standing around in all their glories. The pile of clothing on the floor looked like a rummage sale.

The waiting men hooted and laughed in chorus, pointing and waving. Only about twenty-five feet separated the combatants. I sat down in a chair and beckoned to Gekko who was standing by, watching with a certain amount of satisfaction.

"Give them the silver pill," I commanded.

Gekko smiled, glad now of the opportunity to top his visitor from Moscow.

"As luck would have it, Commissar Damonski, the men are already prepared. We have merely to give the signal and they will start. You see, we gave them the pills at nine o'clock and that was just before you arrived. The pill needs only about twenty minutes to become active and effective."

I frowned. The way the men were looking at the women, Katie's homework on the pills didn't look like it was taking.

"Really?" I stalled. "May I see one of these objects?"

He smiled again, dug a hand into his smock and handed me a shining, metallic-looking object. The silver pill. I looked at it, weighed it in my hand and then to his great surprise, popped it into my mouth.

"Commissar!" he shouted, terrified.

"Gekko," I said, pretending to swallow for I had palmed the pill very easily. "I may join the experiment if only to see for myself. But first we shall see how these others perform, eh?" I chuckled and he looked helplessly toward Orkoff, who merely shrugged. You had to humor commissars. "Frankly, Gekko, it is nothing for me to take on at least four or five females a night. If your pill can increase my efficiency, well then, I would say you had something and would be pleased to report as much to Moscow. You understand?"

Gekko swallowed nervously. "Of course. A brilliant notion." He gestured toward the waiting groups of men and women who had fallen now into a strange silence. Katie, from her chair nearby, was frowning at me. But not openly. I wondered why.

Orkoff stared a question at Gekko. Gekko nodded. Orkoff turned to the men and women, raised his arm like a started in a racing meet and then slammed it down, slicing the air like a knife.

"Begin!" he roared, with more loudness than enthusiasm. I guess he still didn't trust the performance of his pill. Which fit into my scheme just fine. I wanted him to doubt. What I hoped he would see might make him doubt enough to write the whole thing off. With my official disapproval to guide him.

But there was no more time for speculation.

The wild scene in front of us had begun, right before our very eyes. Katie's hand stole over to my lap and squeezed my hand. I held it and suddenly she had leaned over to whisper in my ear: *"You can't join the party, Rod! You'll go so good you'll make the pill look too good no matter how the rest louse up! You want to spoil everything—your own plan?"*

I told you she was smart. Now, why hadn't I thought of that? Walrus-moustache must be right. I am too horny for my own salvation. I patted Katie's hand in approval. She had given me another key to victory.

But meanwhile, back in the gym on the floor—

The ten men had stripped off their jockey shorts. Talk about extremes in male anatomy. Oh, they were all solidly muscled, sturdy peasant stock specimens, but never ever have I seen so much extremism in the male shipping department. Five of the men were beginning to advance on their selected girl, each of them so monumentally stiff and swollen and red as to seem cursed rather than blessed. I wasn't too far wrong. In spite of the rapid growth of the principal male tendon, each of the five men looked in pain. Their faces were taut and constricted. Sweat dotted their cheekbones. They moved with great effort, like walking on eggshells. But the women, blinded by the mammoth joy toys, sprang forward with ecstatic shouts of passion. In a flash, five of them had coupled with the five advancing men and there was a sudden blind pinwheeling of flying hair, thighs, breasts and rumps. I wasn't interested in them just then. I kept my attention on the five remaining men.

It was pathetic. Like a Mutt and Jeff paradox. Their five fellow guinea pigs had reached the heights and they were still down in the depths. Not one of them had been able to manufacture a hard-on, despite the proximity of ten naked lovelies, all begging to be milked and bilked of their Glory mounds. Katie's saltpetre had done more than double-cross them. Whatever other secret ingredient the silver pill contained, it had managed to shrivel them up and keep them even below the normal male level. It was pitiful. These men cursed, looked at the women, cursed again, and in desperation began to masturbate to get an erection. It was hopeless, though, and the remaining five women rushed forward to help. Almost angry, a little dismayed, but sure they could get things going again.

In the middle of this odd scene, other strange things happened. The five dolls trying to copulate with the five big boys were starting to scream and cry out in disappointment. I looked. It was amazing. Not one of the men could get his out-sized tool *in* where it was supposed to do the most good. The women were threshing furiously, widening their legs as much as they could but nothing seemed to help. Unless I was sadly mistaken, all five of the big boys were crying and whimpering in pain. It *hurt*. There was a great gnashing of teeth, hoarse feminine shouts in Russian and Czech that spoke volumes. Nobody on that gym floor was getting what they wanted. The women were more than able and ready, but the five guys with the biggest equipment were as useless as the five guys busting their balls to get something going. Whatever Katie had done, she had done it well.

Operation Silver Pill was a flop.

The inevitable happened. The women, over-yearning, over-prepared, and now let down, turned ugly. They snarled, cursed, jabbed with their hands at lifeless private parts and poked fun at huge erections that were meaningless. The men, all of them, backed away in terror. The big guys in great pain, the little ones hopelessly cowed and ashamed. It broke my heart in five places to see such a terrible scene played out. Men without women. Women without men. And nobody getting their boots laced or ashes hauled or pipes cleaned properly. For a man like me, it was a scene from Hell. A very bad scene.

Now, the groups of tens in the center of the room turned into a feverish riot. The men with grotesque erections turned tail and ran, heading for the door and freedom. The women raced after them, craning their snatches,

143

holding out their breasts, and their poor victims, still painfully clutching their own freakish extensions, bolted from the room. The tiled corridor echoed with shouts, screams and the thunder of running feet. Orkoff had tried to stop them, shouting for order, but they bowled on by him, knocking him down like a tenpin. He rose, spluttering and staggering. I had a mental picture of the five broads chasing the five big-peckered men all over the countryside, screaming for them to be men and do the right thing.

As for the five puny Betchnikians, their women had them cornered in one section of the room. They were spitting out their wrath, kicking with their feet, aiming boldly for the inferior-sized section of the body where they had built their hopes so high. The poor bastard men were all shrinking back in fear. By my side, Gekko was almost in tears, alternately mopping his forehead and muttering under his breath. I took the opening and poured more oil on his troubled waters.

"So, Gekko, this is how you waste the Kremiln's budget! I have seen enough. You will go to your office immediately and draw up a closing report. I want this foolishness ended at once. I have no more time to waste."

"But, Commissar! This is Number Seventy-Nine, a new stage—I can't explain what has happened. It has never reacted like this before——"

"*Backfired* is what you mean! Gekko, do as I have ordered you. It is the only way to escape Siberia."

He shuddered then he looked at me hopelessly.

"The pill you took, Commissar—do you feel a sudden quickening of the blood, a hardening of the arteries—"

"No," I said firmly. "In fact, I feel quite listless and dull. In truth, not even sight of these splendid Betchnikians—the females, of course—has aroused me. I warn you. If your pill has harmed me in any way so that I cannot again enjoy a woman—well, Gekko—make out your report and send it to Moscow. Take Orkoff with you. I will manage the rest of these peasants."

Gekko turned pale. "No, no. You will be all right, Commissar. I assure you. Whatever the pill is, it wears off—heh, heh—would I do anything to harm my Commissar?"

144

Orkoff came over and Katie stood up and straightened her skirt. A thin smile tugged at her lips, but the two scientists couldn't see it. All they could see was the doom of the silver pill project, the bad report card they had to turn in to Moscow, and the snowy prospects of Siberia. They huddled together, crying in each other's beards, and I pushed them toward the door.

"Go," I commanded. "And sin no more in the name of Moscow."

Behind us, the five angry peasant women had just about beaten their victims to the floor of the gymnasium. I could hear the men all begging for mercy. Gekko and Orkoff were beyond caring. Arm-in-arm, they lurched for the doorway and stepped through, sobbing. I motioned to Katie and she ran up the slight incline of ramp and bolted the door and locked it.

She came back, breathless, laughing, gurgling with joy.

"It worked, dammit, it worked. Gee willies, I still know my onions in the lab."

"Never mind that now. You speak the language. Go rescue those five guys, tell the dames the party isn't over yet, and get the men out."

"What are you going to do?" Her mood changed and suspicion flared in her eyes. "Listen. You can't have a private party in here. Gekko and Orkoff could come back——"

"Do it," I snapped, "or no Hollywood and no more Rod. Get me?"

I don't know how she did it but she did it. She growled in her throat, separated the angry dames from the frightened men, got them out in a hurry and they ran for their lives, not even stopping for their jockey shorts. Some of them were bleeding profusely from scratches, kicks and bites. I'm telling you. You disappoint a dame that's ready for action, and sometimes it's like signing your own death warrant. Katie locked the door again after they had gone. The women, sullen and still mad and impatient, sneered at me in my uniform. What the hell could I do? A Bolshevik!

Part of my conceit and mastery is my liking for surprising women. I said nothing. Hoping Katie had said it all. I undressed quickly and when I stepped out of my

145

boots, the five women fell down on their knees in gratitude. Katie said, *"Hmmph!"* and turned around and folded her arms. She didn't want to look, the jealous hussy. I didn't care. It had taken me a great amount of will power to keep my control up and my family jewels on ice while ten splendid Betchnikian maids all drooled for some action from lesser men. Well, I had five all to myself now and the time was ripe for my favorite of all sports. Making maids.

The way Dame Fortune smiled on me sometimes was a public scandal. Not one of the five nudes encircling me now with real hunger in their faces was one of the lusty dolls from the storehouse-in-the-rain orgy. Maybe these were all virgins, to boot!

Anyway, I didn't have time to think about it. Katie had turned her back so she was of no immediate use. I tried to organize the ladies into some sensible kind of arrangement so I could service all five of them, democracy style, but they had been remorselessly teased too long by all the nonsense in that gymnasium that morning. Even as I held up my hands and started to say, "Girls, gorgeous girls, now we will—" the mad cycle began.

It would have frightened any mere mortal.

All five of the naked lovelies sort of growled in their throats like animals, then merged in a tidal wave of fleshly goodies and literally charged toward me. On the fly, arms out, legs gesticulating, hips and all rounded things pumping. I smiled, stood my ground, and met them head-on. It was a Damon Delight, all the way. What five women could take what I had to give and knew how to use? I didn't come by my expertise by doing nothing but reading. I had *lived*. And he who has lived and loved and run away, lives to love another day. And way. But I don't only paraphrase the Ancients for a hobby. I really believe my credos. I do *not* believe in silver pills.

In a furious five seconds, the women had piled into me and the show was on. It was noisy, tumultuous and pure fun. The Betchnikian women, stunned at the sight of my secret weapon, now wanted to make certain it was not a will-o'-the-wisp. A mirage. A nothing. They attacked it *en masse*, fighting for handholds, an encounter, a lay.

I did not disappoint them. I'm sure they would have killed me if I had.

So I went to work with all my all-time, old-time fire and brisk enthusiasm. Ferrago, the Latin from Manhattan, had once watched me sport myself with ten women, and when the action was at its highest and he was taking notes down like mad, the stocky sexologist, who had introduced Cafe Society in the Thirties to the art of *Soixante-Neuf*, had shouted at the top of his voice: *"If you can't lick Mr. Damon, you must surely join him!"*

Vive Ferrago. He had the right idea. I wish he had been alive to see me balling the Jacquelines in Betchnika!

For five assaulting females, there is only one answer. The male must take the initiative or be murdered and ruined forever in the sack league. So I was aggressive and punishingly, sweetly effective, with no holds barred.

I let the first woman reach me, speared her from a standing position and ran her back across the floor. She gagged on my weight and her pals had to stop in their tracks and reverse direction. Too late. By that time I had dragged my woman back with me, dropped to the floor and held her on high, whacking away with measured stroke. Before I let her lie, I rolled to one side, dragging another hungry one to the floor. I had thwacked her three times before she knew what hit her and released all her energies. The remaining three now scrambled for positions and I allowed them to lower away on all parts of my body, knowing I could shake them off at any time. I could too. They were all so open, so ready and aching to be filled, it was like shooting apples in a barrel. These women had so much to give and absolutely no inhibitions at all. So I rolled merrily, plunging free-style, with all available entry points at my disposal. Frontal, rear and facial. Each orifice was a soft retreat from the thorny side of life. What larks! I remained powerfully rigid, hummingly in tune and my flesh seemed to zing in the cool air of the gym. One of the lovelies must have learned some English somewhere because in the midst of this glorious daisy chain someone shouted: *"Hot dog!"* And a few unprintable remarks that never make the family magazines.

I didn't care. The silver pill mission was accomplished.

147

Gekko and Orkoff, thoroughly hoodwinked, were in their offices, drawing up the report that put the kiss of death on the project. I could leave Betchnika anytime now. Walrus-moustache would be proud of me. Ditto the Thaddeus X. Coxe Foundation, and I'd even managed to take care of Christina Ketch, the MVD murderer of twenty-five harmless old geezers. Life looked beautiful again. Especially on the floor of that gym, surrounded by lovely churning rumps and thighs and feverish Glory Mounds all bristling and participatory. What Coxeman could ask for anything more? I had the world by the balls.

Did I ever?

"Bing-bang-boom!" blurted the Americanized Betchnikian female from somewhere under the gorgeous pile. Someone else was nibbling the end of me with all the fervor reserved for blowing the bugle. Another had at my rump, laving her tongue up and down the dirt road like she was trying to macadamize it. I was busy too. I found some pleasant pastures to frolic in, pausing now and then to suck of the delicious fruit hanging in the gardens. And then my spurting goods would bathe the daisy chain with some pure golden liquid. And all the ogling and gobbling ladies, who were with me all the way, would *oooh!* and *aaah!* and I would quicken and thicken to even greater heights. I was in my glory. These poor underprivileged Betchnikian maids had brought out the best in me. I felt like a mission worker whose efforts are blessed because of their altruistic nature. Peace be with you, brothers and sisters!

I had all but forgotten about Katrina Walsky. But she hadn't forgotten about me. Either that, or she was just a lousy *voyeur* with no staying power. Suddenly, in the midst of all the spinning and funmaking, her wrathfully lovely face showed in the medley of faces and bodies, close to my own.

"Bastard!" she hissed.

"Katie, darlin'!" I said.

"Bum!" she snarled.

"Ah, Katie, don't be a killjoy—"

"Whoremaster!" she cried. *"What was I supposed to do? Stand around again and watch you take temperatures with that goddamn thermometer of yours—?"*

148

She was mad but her eyes were shining and the fever had her too. So I reached out and silenced her, the best way I could. I took her own temperature and no woman has ever responded so hotly to the instrument going in. For good measure and extra pleasure, I drove it up at Yankowski's love angle. Katie moaned on high. It sounded like a blues note. The other women, impelled by the sound to greater effort, redoubled their strokes and in no time at all, the seven of us had made very good use of the large floor area of the gymnasium. The walls echoed with our symphony of sex. Everybody had fun but I gave Katie a little extra. I had to. I liked her a helluva lot better and the five other dolls were strangers, after all. Fair's fair.

Later on, the power play took its toll. One by one, with great moaning sighs and grunts of utterly spent and exhausted flesh, the women rolled off me and crawled into various corners of the room to nurse their wounds. The pack thinned until there was only my Katie and me. She liked that. With each departing, sated maid, Katie added a fresh kick to her twitch and shake of the dice. I responded in kind. Finally, we worked up a neat snarl in the center of the floor; and the five women, as tired and fulfilled as they were, watched like students in a rehearsal hall.

Katie gave the performance of her newly discovered sexual life. She hung on, gave as good as she got and even added a few virtuoso licks and flourishes to the occasion. In a fast and furious fusion that lasted another half-hour longer, our *pas de deux* ended with both of us locked in a very artistic French pretzel. The Betchnikian women couldn't help themselves. One by one they applauded. Softly and with great reverence and affection.

The orgy was done.

And the next thing on the agenda was to clear out of the Firnl Lab in a hurry. So everybody got dressed, all nice and gussied again, and we marched toward the locked door. Katie was humming again. And her arm was linked in mine. The five maids were all hushed and quiet. Deep calm had settled over them. So it was a nice orderly retreat, all in all.

In the corridor, the women marched ahead of us and

waved before they disappeared through the front door.
I had timed it just right. For Gekko and Orkoff were
coming down the hall, still like frightened school children,
anxious to make amends with teacher.

"Commissar," Gekko mumbled. "We are working on
the report and will have it ready by tonight for mailing."

"Good, good." I decided to be big about it. I clapped
Gekko and Orkoff on their backs and nearly caved them
in. "Be of good cheer, gentlemen. Moscow will find some
other use for your services. When I make my oral report
to the Kremlin, I shall speak highly of your cooperation.
My word on that."

The sun came up in both their faces. Their beards
seemed to gleam with happiness. Siberia vanished from
their considerations.

"Would you?" they chorused. "That is good of you,
Commissar!"

"Tut," I said. "It is nothing. I, Damonski, am a fair
man if I am nothing. Good day, gentlemen. Comrade
Katrina will drive me to the border where I shall meet
my special car. Hail and farewell!"

"Hail!" said Gekko.

"And farewell!" bleated Orkoff. Katie stuck her hand
to her mouth to stifle a giggle.

We turned our backs on them and walked through the
front doors of the Firnl Laboratory. Behind us I could
hear Gekko muttering to Orkoff. "You see, Orkoff? Devil
take the silver pill . . . it is too undependable. Now we
can ask Moscow if they will let us continue our project
on the sexual behaviour of animals. That would be far
more practical and reliable. . . ."

I could hear no more. I steered Katie toward the Daimler which stood remote and important-looking on the
driveway. The sun was boiling down from the heavens.
A hot day coming. A very hot day. But nothing as torrid
as the morning just spent by Damon and Company.

I had rewritten Betchnikian history.

"What do we do now?" Katie murmured, walking at
my side toward the Daimler.

"Walk," I said, "do not run to the nearest exit."

"Then what, Lover?"

"You wake your father up. Tell him he fell asleep and

in his snooze, he missed the visit of the great Commissar Damonski from Moscow. He'll be disappointed, but at least you'll be covered if Gekko and Orkoff mention me before they clear out of here. You dig?"

"I dig you," she said. "And I don't care about Hollywood or fame or anything anymore. Couldn't you take me with you forever? I'd be your secretary; I type like mad, and I'm good at dictation and all. Besides, didn't you notice how well I filled in when I had to? I get jealous, sure, but I'd never get mad enough to cut it off you or anything stupid like that."

"Katie, you're a peach, but I'm a lone wolf."

"Isn't that the turtle's ass?" she said vehemently. She whipped open her door of the Daimler, and I climbed into the back seat. She wasn't humming anymore. A bad sign.

"Katie."

"Yeah?"

"I'll make a deal with you. The Hollywood bit still stands. But if you drove me to Munich in this heap we could have a ball along the way until I took my plane. We could be together at least another day. As soon as it takes off, I will leave, but I don't mind telling you I am going to miss you like crazy. You're a great lay, Katie. One of the greatest."

"Honest?" Her eyes blinked like moons in the rearview mirror.

"Honest. I wouldn't kid a future rock and roll star like you, would I?"

"Oh, Rod!"

"Well? Coming to Munich with me or not?"

She nodded rapidly. "As soon as we take care of Poppa —gee willies, Rod, I've always wanted to shack up on a trip with a man—and it being you just about makes it perfect!"

I leaned back against the seat cushions and closed my eyes. I felt just fine. My body never better. My mind was at ease, definitely. Global world peace had been restored and there would be no silver pill nonsense to louse up the bivouac. And I could get back to the university and continue the happy life among my test tubes and females, without interruption. Meanwhile, en route to that happy destination, I would have the willing and wanton company of the greatest undiscovered piece of musical property outside of America.

K-K-K-Katie!

So round, so firm, so fully stacked.

So in love with me and what I had.

As Katie herself would say, Gee Willies, I had it made!

The Masters-Johnson people, no matter how technical they ever got on sexual response patterns and truisms, would never understand the Rod Damons of this world. Or the Katrina Walskys.

Some people—if you must know the truth—just would rather get laid than do anything else.

CHAPTER FIFTEEN

Twenty-four hours later, I was back in Munich, with my new luggage, and waiting for the plane in the airport terminal. I was taking the twelve fifteen flight out of Munich for America. Katrina Walsky was on her way back to Betchnika in the Daimler, taking the phony commissar's uniform with her to return to the little theater property building. It had served its purpose.

Our parting was brief and tearless. Katie learned fast. Besides which, she didn't have the strength to cry. We had paused and dallied in every cottage hotel along the route and tangoed together at every opportunity. Once, during a rainstorm, we parked the Daimler in a copse of trees and really went to town. I never realized how much the automobile is conducive to sexual relations. A naked Katie in a car was a revelation. She pulled out all the stops.

And then some.

By my count, when we reached Munich, I'd say we had spent some ten of the twenty-four hours in the sack. Now that is some puning even by my standards. For a recently discharged virgin, it was incredible. Katie was an ace girl all the way. I made her a gift of the Renault.

But Munich came and with it goodbye.

I kissed her in the airport terminal. I didn't want her

152

to wait until the plane took off. She understood. She was a sweetheart right to the end.

"So long, Katie. See you in Hollywood."

"Bye, Rod. It's *been.*

"And it will *be.*"

We kissed again.

"Katie, do me a favor?"

"Anything, lover."

"Say Gee Willies again and beat it."

So she did and walked out of my life, through the revolving doors and her adorable rump twitched and revolved all the way. Never mind the future before her—she would always have a great future behind her.

I knew I was going to miss her, but in my business, the beach is loaded with pebbles. I would make sure however when I got back stateside that Walrus-moustache would keep his promise and get Katrina Walsky out of that hick nowhere known as Betchnika.

With some time to burn, I called the tall trim bastard on the special phone and made my report. He listened with all his yeah-team-spirit, and when I was done, he fairly crowed from his end of the line.

"Magnificent, Damon!"

"Yeah, sure."

"Superlative!"

"Uh huh."

"Splendid!"

"If you say so."

"You have dealt that silver pill project a death blow from which it will never recover——"

"Cut the crap. Can I come home now? I'm tired. I want to get back to my university. And Suzanne and Annette. They're sisters who—oh, hell, forget it."

He chuckled, in his own lionizing way.

"Still feathering your nest, eh, my boy? You are the eighth wonder of the world. When will you run dry—?"

"When the Montreal Expos win the pennant," I snapped. "Like never. And for another thing—"

Suddenly, through the glass door of the booth I saw a familiar sight. A trim figure, with a rump swinging like a pendulum, a high shelf of breast, but this time there was no airline uniform. No blue outfit. It couldn't be, but

153

it was. Wilhelmina of Lufthansa. But not in mufti. And she was heading down the sloping ramp toward the doors leading out to the field. There was no time to lose.

"I say, Damon," Walrus-moustache purred, "are you still there?"

"But not for long. So long, pal. See you in the funny papers!"

He exploded, I hung up and then I broke the four-minute mile leaving the booth and catching up with the lovely phantom just reaching the glass doors. Out on the field, beyond the wire fences, great big planes shone on the runway. Jet engines blasted the Munich sky. It was a fine day to go winging off in all directions. Why not?

I grabbed her by the buttocks, she stiffened, and whirled on me, almost dropping her luggage. Which I now saw consisted of a set of bound skis and shoes and a neat blue flight bag.

It was her all right.

Eyes as blue as ink, skin like sapphires winking and that oh so great over-all blondeness. Her red mouth dropped when she recognized me, to be replaced by a bronze flush of pure loveliness.

"Wilhelmina of Lufthansa!" I said.

"Damon of America!" she blurted.

We embraced. Almost immediately my temperature soared. She felt it, knew it and hugged me even tighter.

"But this is marvelous," she crooned. "What are you doing here? I thought you'd forgotten me and gone back to your America."

"Who me? Nonsense. Never happen. As it does happen, my affairs are concluded in Munich and I thought it might be nice to try the skiing in St. Moritz?"

The question almost didn't need an answer.

"Oh, Rod. This is too much—that is exactly where I am going—this is a heavenly coincidence! I have the entire weekend at my disposal and it would be marvelous if we could spend it together—"

"We will." I took her arm, changing my plans on the spot. The good old U.S.A. could do without me for another Friday, Saturday and Sunday. This was one weekend that would not be Lost. And if all went as well as I expected, Wilhelmina would have a *nice weak end* when

154

I was through with her. "I'm yours until Monday, Willie."

Skiing, sheing, it's all the same to me.

If they want to mix it up with snow and ice and mountains, it's okay with me.

Wilhelmina, *sympatico* Willie, stood in awe of our chance meeting. It seemed God-like to her that we should run into each other. Ships that pass in the night seldom do, ever again. She knew that much, with her airline time and experience.

We waited in the alcove by the doorway as our plane thrummed up on the runway. I'd managed to run and go get a new ticket for the flight. Wilhelmina's flight was still fifteen minutes off. She had wanted to go on board earlier to see some of her old pals on the flight. She knew the crew.

So we held hands in the alcove and talked and her eyes continued to stray down toward my crotch. I caught her looking and laughed. "It's still there, lovely. All in one piece."

Wilhelmina shook her head, sighing.

"It still is amazing. After we—on the plane—I must confess—I tried to make love to another man—but it was no use. He was so small, so puny—I'm afraid I was a very naughty woman. I laughed at him and walked out. You see, you have spoiled me for other men. It was meant that we should meet like this. It is Kismet."

Dames are a romantic breed, aren't they?

"Let me spoil you some more, huh?"

"I would like that. Yes." She lowered her hands so no one could see and gave a gentle squeeze to that which makes me tick. Her eyes jumped.

"Himmel!" she gasped. "It is always like that?"

"Always. Even more so when the woman is right."

"And I am right?"

"If you were any righter, Willie, they'd arrest you for subversion. I can't wait to get to St. Moritz."

She chuckled. A woman's chuckle. I had missed something."

"What's funny?"

"We won't have to wait until St. Moritz. It will be fine in the Alps, but we won't have to wait—you will see."

155

I saw.

On the flight.

Even though it was broad daylight and a short trip, Wilhelmina's pal, the stewardess, managed to give us the rearmost window seat, which was curtained and private. It was the spot reserved for the stews and crew to grab a smoke if they wanted to. I tell you—virgins learn fast if they are broken in properly. Obviously I had broken Wilhelmina in properly. We had no sooner left Munich below the cloudbanks of fluff and cotton, that she immediately unzippered my fly for a look at the family jewels. It was the very first thing she insisted on doing. I thrilled to her touch and towered another few inches in response.

"Hey," I murmured. "I am glad to see you but don't rush me. I'm swelling—" She wasn't listening. Her golden head went down and her red mouth encircled me. Softly, slowly and with great affection. She murmured happily in her throat. I sat back, made myself comfortable and fastened my right hand around her superbly curved rump, managing to insert a deft hand under her skirt between the hills of home. My most very favorite territory in all female topography.

This was even better than anything in Betchnika.

Wilhelmina had willowy, filled-out height. Katrina Walsky hadn't. It does make a slight, very fine difference in the leg department.

She kissed me once.

She kissed me twice.

And then she kissed me again.

I got longer and longer. Soon she had to see to it that both her hands held the beautiful monster at bay. I didn't let go, though. I was having too much fun.

She *mmmmmmed* and *ummmmmmmed* and *yummed* and my busy hand made her begin to twitch and strain and flutter. Her long thighs parted and even the drone of the jet engines could not drown out her sighs. She was giving milk like a prize Holstein cow.

"Oh, Rod. . . ."

It was a whisper. A plea.

"Yeah, Willie?"

"Let go. Please. Release yourself. Don't hold back.

Always I have wanted to feel you pulsate in my mouth
. . . *please?*"

What's a guy to do with a doll like that except to accommodate her and do exactly what she wants? I nodded,
waited and just as her red lips seemed to sheath me as
far as it could, I cut loose. The full golden tide. The
Milky Way. The pathway to the stars and the outer space
of male sexual bliss. It was a long time coming and a
long time going. But I did not faze the maiden of the
skies. If anything, she drank and chewed me to a fare-
thee-well, and soon we were clasped together warmly and
I was locked inside where it was nice and warm. The
steady rhythm of the plane lulled us. But not for long.

"Lover," she said simply. "Man of mine. Now will you
do what I ask of you . . . *please?*"

"Ask me anything."

"Then drink the Rhinemaiden, Damon darling, and
then take her for she is yours. Here in the bold blue sky
she loves, and up here in the sun where she lives. . . ."

Geezis, it was poetry.

In motion and in flight.

Wilhelmina looked at me, smiled her red-lipped smile
and I gently urged her creamy thighs apart and lowered
myself away to the waiting Paradise whose gates were
covered with the magnificent ivy that Mother Nature put
there and man can never match or manufacture in a laboratory. Any laboratory. The Venus Mound bows to
nothing in the beauty league.

'Twas ever thus. Thanks to Jalal al-Din al-Siyuti, Yankowski, Dealey, Nakoma, Saganelli, Von Firtz, Von Tappen, Ferrago, and all that marvelous crew, who really
understood women.

Quixotic Rod Damon too, who perhaps understands
them better than anybody. Ask my girls at the university.
Ask anything in skirts who has ever had the pleasure of
my company.

Wilhelmina shrieked with discovery.

"*Oh, oh, oh . . . Rod . . . you are coming to the cabaret . . . to St. Moritz . . . you will take me on skis, off
skis, on the ski-lift . . . oh, oh, oh. . . .*"

You know that dame promised me just about everything all the way on the flight into St. Moritz.

You know something else?

She kept every one of her promises too.

No wonder the Rhineland is coming back as a world power.

Hitler's *Festung Europa* proved to be a myth.

But Germany is having a ball.

Just like Rod Damon, they are putting their money where their mouth is.

Eat, drink and be merry, for tomorrow you may be dead.

With a life campaign like that, how can the Wilhelminas of this world lose?

So much for politics—

Meanwhile, back at Wilhelmina's thighs, I reveled and rocked and rolled all the way into St. Moritz.

I was coming in on a *ring-a-ding-ding* and a bare-assed beauty.

It's the only way to live.

Thus, I refute all bluenoses and killjoys everywhere.

9 780446 543262